Fireflies
and
Chocolate

by

Ailish Sinclair

GWL
PUBLISHING

First Published in 2021
by GWL Publishing
an imprint of Great War Literature Publishing LLP

Produced in United Kingdom

ISBN 978-1-910603-84-0 Paperback Edition

GWL Publishing
2 Little Breach
Chichester PO19 5TX

www.gwlpublishing.co.uk

PUBLISHER'S DISCLAIMER

Due to the historical nature and setting of this novel, some of the language
employed could be deemed offensive. Whilst the publisher recognises the
sensitive nature of the language, it is deemed that this is acceptable, within
the context of the period in which the narrative is set.

Dedication

To all the children who were not cherished as you should have been.

May you find your true families.

Acknowledgements

This book was written while suffering from, and eventually being diagnosed with, an autoimmune disorder. So more gratitude than ever goes out to my family – Davie, Daniel and Charlotte – for their unending support and practical help.

Thanks also goes to Wendy at GWL for encouraging me to enlarge on the good bits and shrink the less than good bits!

And to all the NHS staff – nurses, doctors, paramedics, first responders, receptionists, cooks and cleaners – who helped me in so very many different ways, thank you.
You are amazing.

Chapter One

May 11ᵗʰ 1743

"Ach, but will you look at that? The sheer and utter boredom of it!"

The dull sight in front of us disna worry my companion, Prince Charles of all Scotland and Britain and the world. He's more concerned with sniffing out rabbits and foxes and hedgehogs as he runs along the oak lined path, than he is with staring at old stones.

So many old stones. They're everywhere aroon here. Ahead, there's the ancient circle of tall stones. Behind is the castle, a great pile of pink granite. I hoik up my skirts and climb onto the biggest of the standing stones, the muckle stane as it's called, and stare back doon at the castle. My home. My great big boring pink hame, with its tower and its turrets and its great big empty hall.

Now, I ken fit you'd like to say to me: "Elizabeth Manteith, you're a spoilt wee lassie. Fit most folk wouldna give to live in a castle."

Aye, well. You dinna ken. You dinna ken at all.

I sit down and pick at a bit of lichen, all grey and hard and sprigly. That's my life here, you see. Grey. Hard. Sprigly. I pick another bit of lichen off. And another and another, as if I can lay the stone bare and make everything new. But I canna. The task is soon abandoned and I lie down on the stone. As if dead. As if laid out all neatly in a tomb. Which I might as well be. Like my wee brother. In heaven.

I listen to the rustling sounds between the trees as Prince Charles tries to persuade the wildlife to play with him, but he soon grows bored, like me, and runs back into the circle, barking and yipping beside the great stone until I lift him up to sit atop it. I turn the spaniel to look west, far out over the trees and fields, and wee hoosies and farms, to where the sky shows red. I once attended grand shows and plays in London with my father. We would drink chocolate in a coffee house together before going to the theatre. He's far too busy for that now, so this is what we have, me and Prince Charles. It's a good one though, this show in the heavens; there's purple and white all in among the red, a bit of dark swirling blue. I stand up and the wind takes my hair and blows it all forwards towards the colours in the sky, red meeting red in the air.

And then: the change. It's swift. The bright colours fade and are replaced with dark blue. Really dark blue. And all across the land, or so it seems, wee golden lights come on in the wee hoose windows. Like fireflies. Exotic bugs from faraway places. I've read about them, both the flies and the faraway lands. I reach out my arms and wish I could fly away. To adventure. To fun. To laughter and life and warmth. And maybe, just maybe, somewhere out there might be… true love? I've read about that too.

The sky darkens to grey, real fast, and the lights no longer look like fireflies, just windows in houses, lit for the night.

"Aye, well. Chance would be a fine thing," I tell Prince Charles as I jump down and lift him back to the ground too. It's a saying I hear just about every day. It's Eppy's standard answer to all suggestions of ways to make life a bit mair exciting. But it's not what she says today, not on this dark and dismal eve, as we walk into the kitchen looking for a bite to eat.

"Oh, Miss Elizabeth!" she says. "Look at your fine dress."

This is not a true description of my garment. It's been a long time since I wore a 'fine dress'. This one is old. This one is brown. The mud on it makes little difference to its appearance.

"Ye ken I'll have to wash it oot noo," says Eppy.

Well, that is true. "I'll help," I offer, though laundry is not one of my best skills. I'm better at cooking.

We come to an agreement. Eppy washes out the skirt with her strong old woman hands and I prepare 'a wee sup of supper' for us all, 'us all' being Eppy and me and Old Jock, Eppy's husband. They've something to tell me after supper, says Eppy as I select the best looking onion to make a simple broth. I've to sit doon and have a talk with them, apparently. It'll be about my room again. The sheer and utter state of it. The books all over the floor. The clothes flung off and not picked up. The ashes from letters I sometimes burn in the fire; the last one, from my father, about him not coming home for my birthday later in the year as planned because he's so busy furthering the cause. That one floated about in smokey shreds and left black marks on the rug. A draught came down the chimney. And that's not my fault. And who's going to see it anyway? Who's going to ken? No one; that's who. And I slice up the onion real fast.

"Now you can just wipe that scowl off yer bonny face," says Jock after we've eaten our broth and cheese and bread. "Ye've sixteen years on you now; it's time to stop acting like a wee bairn, even though you still look like one."

I glance at the ceiling briefly and then look back at him and wait. I'm annoyed about looking younger than I am and am most aggrieved that Jock chooses to mention it now, when he's about to chastise me for the mess of my room, as if I am actually a child. That has to be what this is. I dinna think it'll be about me and Prince Charles making noise on the big stairs and disturbing mamma again. We've been more careful about that recently.

"There's been a letter come from your father," he says. "With money for a bigger horse for you."

I open my mouth, but am too astonished to speak. I mean, I outgrew the little pony years ago but I never thought I'd get a replacement. I never thought anyone would even think about it. But they have. *He* has.

And we're going out tomorrow! To Aberdeen! I'm getting to choose a horse! I'm going to see people and the sea, and people and ships, and so many horses, and the things that come off the ships there and the things that go on, and all the other things they sell in the market! It's the most exciting thing to happen in my life since, well, a long time. Since before Thomas died. And mother took nae weel. Since before all of that.

"Now, I think you should let Jock go by himself," says Eppy, as if such an unthinkable event could ever be allowed to happen. "He knows horses, and Aberdeen is not a safe place for young quines."

"Eppy, I'll be fine. And I'm choosing my own horse. You said that's what the letter said I could do."

"Aye…"

Ha! She canna argue with my father, the Laird of this place, especially when he's not here. But she does tell a long tale of her cousin's neighbour's daughter's lad from Huntly, that went into Aberdeen to look for work and has never been seen or heard from since.

"I'm nae some daftie fae Huntly," I tell her.

"But ye'll stay right next to Jock the whole time."

I agree. Aye. I'll nae stray. Prince Charles is coming with me too. And I'm getting a new horse. I'll be able to ride out, far out, to the west or any other way that I fancy to take. To the sea. And the hills. To places that are not here. To adventure. And fun. And, I ken you think I'm silly for it, but you never know, true love could be out there somewhere too.

Chapter Two

I'm far too excited to sleep. I'm so, so awake. Prince Charles is too. He lies on top of the bed clothes, bright eyes watching me, alert for potential walks and mischief. I rub his floppy ears; I can still see the black and white and gold of his fur. It's not sheer and utter darkness tonight. It never is in summer here. And it's almost summer. It's almost the day of going out. That's it. No sleep for me.

I get up and pull my favourite green plaid around myself. It's an old fashioned thing to wear, but it's thick and soft and warm and just what I need to wander about the draughty castle. Down the winding stairs I go. Into the great hall. The twelve tall windows let in a little of that Scottish summer night-time silvery light and I imagine that it's back in the day, my younger days, the olden days. Golden days? Fitever. A time of parties and balls and fine ladies with bonny dresses and fine gentlemen done up in all their fancy clothes with buckles on their shoes.

I curtsey to my invisible suitor. He bows. And we dance round the room, Prince Charles following on, his tufty wee paws tip-tapping across the wooden floor behind me. I stop at the fireplace, and my dancing partner evaporates into the dark shadows of the room. I run my fingers over the wooden carvings of the mantle. The flowers. The three plums. These plump fruits have great meaning. To those that understand. They let the guests know where the castle's loyalties lie. With the one true king. And with his son, the bonny Prince himself.

I lifted Thomas up to see the plums once and explained it all to him. He laughed. I remember that sound and how it made me feel, all happy and light and tickly inside. I remember it but I dinna feel like that now. I never do. But tomorrow. Ah, tomorrow. I'll be away from here. And who can ken what fortune awaits me? Who can ken who might be in Aberdeen? Many a fine gentleman with buckles on his shoes. Maybe even a prince! A prince who might fall into deep and desperate love with a wee lassie from a castle in just one glance! I laugh out loud at my own daftness and it echoes high up in the ceiling.

I do want the best of luck tomorrow though. For unlikely things like meeting princes, but also for likely things like finding the best horse. So I tiptoe back up the stairs. No noise tonight in my soft knitted bed socks. No disturbing mamma. Right up I go, round and round the stairway, until I come to the very top room, my father's room. The door opens easily and I slip inside. It's all the same in here; it never changes. The big bed with the Mermaid and the Bear. My great, great, great, great, great − I can never remember how many greats − grandparents. Oh aye, I'm related to a mermaid, so maybe my storybook imaginings might have some chance of coming true?

It's something of hers I need now as I slide open a drawer and take out the small key, slipping it into the tiny keyhole on the floor as I kneel to open the door to the Priest's hole. Down in there are hidden the family secrets; my father showed it to me once as a place for hiding if ever that be needed. But I saw all the other things and I came back later on my own. To look. And touch. And read. I read the writings of Isobell Manteith, the mermaid; many a terrible thing did happen to her. Especially in Aberdeen. They accused her of being a witch. But that disna go on noo. I winna need luck in that regard at least.

I feel about on the floor for something I hid here myself, the faint light not extending itself all the way into the depths of the floor, and I find it. My mermaid grandmother's pin. An elfin blade that was cast in silver for her to wear as a brooch. Now, truth be told, according to what she wrote, it maybe didna bring her the best of luck, but it's always been good to me. She buried it in the stone circle, so say her writings, and I found it there when I was a very wee lassie. It came up in a molehill while I was dancing aboot in the circle. I saw movement in the mound of earth and there it sat, glinting in the sun. I didn't know what it was then, of course. Eppy said it was a gift from the fairies, just for me. My father said it was a carved arrowhead from long ago. People used to put silver round them and wear them for luck. I like to think that Eppy's right. That it is just for me. I mean, lots of Manteiths must have read the story over the years and known about the blade and where it was buried, and maybe some of them looked for it? But the circle only gave it up for me.

I took it to London years ago where we did have the most merry of times. I took it to our island lands in the west and there was much happiness to be had there too. I hid it here under the floor to stop my nasty cousin Matthew finding it and taking it for his own. So the elfin blade was down here in the dark when Thomas took his fit and died. He was only two years old. And it's been here ever since. It's time for it to come out into the light of day and bring luck to the Manteiths again. I pin it to my plaid and the silver casing catches a wee bitty of light from the windows. Even the grey stone of the old arrow shines in its own stony way.

I curl up on the big bed and go to sleep for a while after all. But I'm still up long afore Eppy and Jock. I light the fire in the kitchen. I put on the porridge and eat mine before they come through. Then I run upstairs to brush the worst tangles out of my hair, before Eppy can tell me to do anything else that might delay the adventure, and put on my finest gown. It does not have a hoop. I have wanted a hooped gown for a long long time. The fun I could have with it, running up and down the stairs! Swaying it from side to side. And generally looking most affa grand and bonny. But, no matter. A horse will do fine to be going on with. I put my plaid back on too, for travelling, pinned with the Elfin Blade, and am all ready to go before the sun is properly risen.

"You'll be going to say goodbye to your Mamma," says Eppy, looking me up and down as I wait for Jock to be ready.

"I would not want to disturb her," I say.

Eppy shakes her head. "She's clearer today; you's look in afore you go."

Damn. I shouldna curse. But, damn. I mutter it under my breath as I walk up the stairs. Damn, damn, damn, damn. Step, step, step, step. It's hard to make my feet walk in that direction when they know where they are headed. And then they want to run past. Up to the top of the tower. I could hide in the Priest's hole! But no: get it over and get gone. That's the way of it. That's what I've got to do.

It's like walking into an evil cloud. The spicy smell, like someone has vomited up a fruitcake and a whole cask of wine. Mamma's drops. To help her forget. To help her bear all she has to bear. Fitever.

"Elizabeth." She speaks. She looks like a wee ghostie there, pale against her pillow. And I swear she gets smaller every time I see her.

"Mamma," I say, and curtsey.

"Oh," she says in a forlorn type of voice, and I know it's not going to be easy or kind today. "You used to be such a bonny wee lass." For a moment she sounds like she might be going to cry. "So dainty. Like a pretty doll. Why have you grown so tall? And your hair so red and curled! You're like a tree that's taken fire in the woods." And then she's laughing. Laughing and laughing. Like a drunken person. Which I suppose she is. I think there's a fair amount of drink in Laudanum.

I walk over and look down at her as she roars and coughs at the sight of me. I lean down into the stink and kiss her cheek. It's all dried up, as if she's dead already. "Goodbye Mamma," I tell her. And then I walk away.

Chapter Three

What a time it takes to get to Aberdeen. It's as well we were all up and about early. Half the day is gone before we finally reach the town and then Jock wants to stop and talk to all these mannies, about the best horses he says, but I don't know, it all seems to be about the weather, which is pretty fine today. I can smell the sea, and fish, and dirt. But somewhere here, among all these grey houses and streets and folk, is the market and my new horse.

Prince Charles smells something too, something for eating, I'll warrant. He's an awful wee dug for chasing food. And he's off, straight away from me, down a narrow side lane, racing across the cobbles, or cassies as they call them in this town, his wee ears flopping up and down as he runs.

"I'll just get him," I call back to Jock as I start to run too. "I'll just be a wee minty."

I hear Jock call my name. "Miss Elizabeth!" And there's some warning about being careful. And possibly waiting for him. But I'm off. Maybe I'll find my perfect horse myself. All by myself. And Jock will be proud of me and he'll tell Eppy about it later. Over supper. But where is Prince Charles? It's busier down this alley than I expected. I dodge men and women and almost trip over a tiny bairn playing right there on the slimy cassies.

I see a flash of black and white and gold as my wee devil of a dog darts round the corner and then it's even busier. We're down at the harbour and the smell of fish is dense in the air, though still not as bad as Laudanum. I'd take rotten fish guts over that any day of the week.

But can I see Prince Charles? I shout his name, realising it's a slightly embarrassing thing to be calling out on a busy dock, and I do get a few queer looks.

"You lost something, lassie?" asks a man. I don't much like the kind of him, he's all sneakit looking round the eyes, but he may have seen Prince Charles. I don't want to be thought of as a rich lady and end up getting robbed by ruffians, so I'm careful nae to speak too properly.

"Aye, my wee dug. Hiv ye seen 'im?"

"Fit's he look like?"

"Sma." I hold my hand down to show the smallness of the spaniel. "Black and white and copper. Floppy ears. Ye ken?"

The man laughs. "He ran onto that ship over there," he informs me, pointing to a three masted cargo boat. "I thought he must be Captain Ragg's new pet." He laughs again, as does another man beside him and they both follow me to the boat.

I don't know what to do. I look round to see if Jock has arrived on the quay but there's no sign of him. And it is fully possible that Prince Charles ran onto this ship. If he smelled food, he'd run just about anywhere. I could maybe ask to see this Captain Ragg, see what's what. So I walk over the gangplank, aware of the sea beneath me. The harbour. My mermaid grandmother was dookit in there. The water looks dirty. Stinky.

And then all there is, is dark stinky bad horribleness. I've been encased! In a sack! I scream and try to lash out at my assailants but then there's only pain, a bursting kind of pain in the back of my head and, even though it's summer in Scotland, everything goes completely dark.

*****

Sheer Dark. Utter Pain. That's my world. I canna see anything, and that alone should make me frightened but it disna. Because I'm really really angry. And for a moment I can't remember why I'm so cross, but I feel around me, looking for Prince Charles. He ran off. I remember that. He ran off, and to where? "Prince Charles!"

"There's nae princes here, quine," says a voice to my left. "Maybe you should open your een and see."

I open my een, my eyes. And oh, do I see.

I'm in a large wooden room with a low ceiling, and there are many many other young folk and bairns and a few wifies in here too, some of them with babies in their arms. There's chairs and tables everywhere, children sitting under them and on them. And the world is moving, swaying right to left and back again all the time. A boat. *The* boat. I walked across the plank. Oh no. Oh no, oh no, oh no. This can't be.

"I have to get off," I call and start to stand up, only to fall back down at once, all dizzy and sick feeling, which is ridiculous because I never get sea sick.

"You're hurt," says that same voice from before. "There's blood in your hair."

I do two things at once: I look round at the boy who's sitting beside me and I touch the back of my head. The boy is sturdy and honest looking, probably about the same age as me, and my head is sore as sore can be. And he's right, the boy, that is: my hair is all crusty with dried blood.

"I was attacked," I remember. "Put in a sack."

"Oh man," says the boy. "You wis kidnapped?"

I nod, still feeling a bit sick.

"I wis kidnapped too," he tells me. "Lots of us has been. We've been held in different places in Aberdeen for months."

"Oh dinna start, Peter," says a plump girl with golden curls, her voice affa loud for my sair heid. "We're bound for a better place. If you've changed your mind about selling your indentures, it's too late now."

"I never sold my indentures," he replies, angry.

"Neither did I," I say, joining him in rage.

"Oh, stop making up stories," says the girl, glancing back towards the door of the room.

"I was beaten about the head and put in here," I tell her, and the whole rest of the large room, that much anger comes out in the words.

"I demand to see whoever is in charge." Memory stirs. "Ragg! I demand to see Captain Ragg and be returned to land at once."

I stand, successfully this time, the boy Peter giving me his arm, and we make our way through the many people to the front of the room. Two men guard the doorway there. Two men that I recognise.

"You!" I say, rage making my voice loud again. "You have kidnapped Lady Elizabeth Manteith of the castle. My father is a Laird and he will see you hang for this." In truth it is my mother who is the Lady and I am a Maid, but the grander title will serve us better here.

"Now, now, Betty," says one of the men, the first that spoke to me before, at the harbour. "Simmer doon."

They laugh their evil laugh again.

"You will return myself, and Peter…" I look at my companion and he nods in encouragement. "You will return us to the quay at once; it is illegal to force innocent people into indenture." Isn't it? It must be, surely.

"Yer dad selt you to us," says the man. "Yer indenture is all signed and sealed by the magistrate. Betty McKay fae Turriff, traded for monies by her drunkard of a pa."

"I am Elizabeth Manteith and I am not from Turriff! Nor is my father a drunkard. He's one of the highest personages in the land."

"Disna really matter," the man tells me. "We're nae on land noo. We're nae in Scotland noo. Yer going to the new world and ye better get used to it. Hae some ship's biscuit and quiet doon Betty, else we'll hae to deal mare harshly wi' you."

He holds out a dirty, stinking, rotten looking bit of chewed hardtack.

I knock it out of his hand and spit at his feet.

Chapter Four

So here I am. In my own wee gaol. And very tiny it is. And very dark. Not too stinky. Dry. Cool. Noisy though. There's the creaking and cracking of the wooden ship around me and the sound of the sea outside. Then there's me crying. I'm a bit ashamed about that. At first I was all fury and fire, fighting with the men and screaming and yelling as they grabbed and pulled and then shoved me in here.

But then my voice grew hoarse. And it was doing no good. I had a feeling they had put me somewhere where no one could hear me. And that's when I thought of Jock and what he must be thinking and feeling. And Eppy. They would be so sad and think themselves so guilty. And Prince Charles. Would anyone ever find him? Would he be fed?

So I'm behaving like a fretty baby. Crying on the floor of this strange and terrible crib. Sobbing so much I can hardly breathe. Jock would search and search for me. Maybe he would find a clue? Maybe someone might have seen me walk – like an idiot – onto this boat? But he would still have to go home to the castle without me and tell Eppy and she would be most affa upset. My howls increase.

Mamma, I dinna worry about. She will not care. And hopefully I can be returned before my father has to know about any of it. Aye. That's it. I need a plan.

The goal: to get home.

But first, I need more information.

Like, where am I headed? The new world, they said. But they surely canna mean the colonies, Virginia and Jamestown, those places? It would take months to get there. No, I'm thinking, and hoping, that the ship is sailing for some remote Scottish island. Must be somewhere that needs workers. Maybe round on the West where I have kin? I can escape, I have no doubt of that; these mannies who guard us are big and rough, but not too clever.

Knocking interrupts my thoughts. And then: "Miss Elizabeth?"

It's the boy, Peter. I recognise his voice. "Aye, I'm in here," I say, glad that I'm no longer crying, and that no one else has to know about that.

"I've a piece for ye," he says. "I'll slide it under the door."

I crouch down and peer through the murk and take hold of the shape that appears in the gap between door and floor.

"It's gingerbread," he says. "We was given it on the first night before we sailed. You was still sleeping then. But I saved a bit."

I raise it to my nose and inhale the spicy sweetness of it. My belly grumbles, being so very empty. "Thank you so very much, Peter," I tell him, embarrassed that my voice trembles like I'm away to cry again.

"They'll let you oot soon," he says. "And we'll just have to be quiet."

"Aye," I agree. He's right about that. Being manhandled and shut in small places will not help me get home. We're in such a serious situation that just surviving this voyage has to be the actual first step of my plan. I take a bite of the gingerbread. And it's so good. Maybe the best thing I've ever tasted in my life. There's a chewy treacly-ness to it as I gobble it up, like something Eppy and me might have made in the kitchen. No. I mustn't think of Eppy. I am here now, and this is what I have to deal with.

"I winna forget this kindness," I tell Peter and he leaves, in case one of the guarding mannies sees him.

I bury my face in my plaid for comfort. The green weave holds hints of home: the fire in the kitchen of the castle, the smell of broth cooking and the soap that Eppy uses to clean most everything, from the table to our hands. The garment also holds the Elfin Blade, a piece of jewellery that might easily be stolen in this place. I move it so it is holding the plaid together on the inside, unseen and safe.

I am Elizabeth Manteith, of the castle, a woman born of a line of strong women, with some exceptions, and I will achieve my goal of going home.

*****

When they come to let me out I offer no complaint. I stand tall and walk back through, quiet as a mouse. I see Peter at the back of the room, which I now realise is the hold of the ship, and I squeeze through the throng of people, many of whom are quite little bairns, to re-join him. There on the floor is the sack that I was captured in. It is my bed now. I sit on it, again with no complaint, and then I whisper to Peter: "Tell me everything you ken about this boat and where it is bound, and for what purpose."

Peter, Peter Williamson as his full name is, kens a lot, having been in captivity for many months and having a good pair of ears on him. We are aboard a vessel called The Planter, bound for the New World and – my heart sinks a bit at this – he does mean the American colonies, specifically Pennsylvania, a place I know nothing about. We are part of the cargo along with the tables and chairs. We, even the youngest of us, are to be sold at the slave market in the city of Philadelphia. It was the merchants and magistrates of Aberdeen who arranged all the kidnappings; Peter saw the Dean of Guild give out wee purses of coins to the rogues himself. We are their latest business deal, a gold mine of free flesh plucked from the streets of Aberdeen.

"I will tell my father all this," I say. "He knows the grand men of Aberdeen and he will see justice done!"

"But Elizabeth," says Peter. "Yer father's getting further away every minute. He canna save us noo."

"No," I agree, this obviously being true. "We have to save ourselves now, then escape and get word to our families and return home."

"Div ye ken fit passage costs, quine?" he asks.

I shake my head. No. I've no idea of that at all.

"Years of work," he explains. "That's why people sell their indentures. A chance at a new life. Passage paid and a bit o' money or land at the end of it. Some of those wifies over there say they sold theirs like that, but I think they're here to keep an eye on us. "

I eye the wifies uncertainly. They do seem to be watching us. Peter could be right. It certainly seems that his bright eyes miss very little.

"Whatever the truth of it," I tell him, "my father will pay for me to come home, and you too, Peter. I told you I wouldna forget your kindness. And I winna."

"Really?" he says, sounding unbelieving. "Yer nae saying you're actually a Lady of a castle? I thought that was just a tale to rile those twa up." He gestures his head back towards the entrance to the hold, and to the ruffians who stand there guarding us.

A girl jumps down from a table beside, the one with the golden curls who spoke to Peter before. "Oh, I kent she wis someone fine," she says. "Look at her gown. She's hiding it under yon blanket thing but you can still see she's nae one of us."

She may have drawn attention to my clothing, indeed everyone is now looking our way, but it's her own attire that draws my eye. It's low cut, no kerchief even for modesty over the bosom. I have no need of a kerchief; Eppy has not let me have such a style of dress as yet. Mine is buttoned high up to my neck under the plaid.

"So, Lady Elizabeth," says the young woman. "Tell us more about yersel."

Children shuffle nearer to hear. The wifies turn their heads our way. Even the villainous guards are listening. I wish I was like my grandmother, the mermaid, who could tell stories. But I can't. I canna think what to say. So I just tell them about the castle.

"It's pink and has a high tower, and a grand great hall, and it's the most beautiful castle in the world."

The girl laughs. "Oh aye?"

"Aye." I nod. It is. "It's surrounded by ancient oak woods. Fallen trees get made into fine furniture, much better than this." I point at the nearby tables. "We have a loch and a stone circle, and many many tenant farms to take care of."

"My, my, we are joined by royalty today, right enough," says the girl and she curtseys to me. Everyone laughs.

"I'm not royalty," I tell her, tell everyone. "I'm just the same as you. A kidnapped prisoner on board a slave ship."

And with that our gaolers descend.

Chapter Five

"She didna mean it," cries the young woman with the low cut dress as the men take hold of my arms. "Elizabeth was just saying that she wants to join me in the fo'c'sle tonight."

"Is that right?" says one of them, looking me up and down but, more importantly, releasing my arm. So I nod, though I've no idea what the 'fo'c'sle' is.

"Aye," says the girl. "We might just take a turn about the deck first though, stretch our legs."

There's a pause. The girl raises her chin and stares the guard down in some sort of defiance or test or communication I don't understand.

They say we can go. We're getting to walk about up on the deck. No guards are to accompany us either. It is the most astonishing turn of events.

Peter lays a hand on my arm as the girl and I make to leave the hold. "You don't want to go to the fo'c'scle Elizabeth," he says in a most serious voice, looking at me rather intensely with his dark brown eyes.

"You should come too," I say.

"That's not going to happen," he tells me, still very intense.

The girl pulls at my other arm and we're off towards the steps. "I can ask if you can join us in the fo'c'sle," I call back to Peter, really not wanting to leave my new friend behind.

He just shakes his head and sort of laughs, but not in a happy way, not in a friendly way. I feel a bit offended to be honest. Is he jealous? He'd seemed so nice and now he's laughing at me?

I climb up the steps behind the girl, determining to leave Peter behind in the hold. For now. I winna desert him entirely. I winna forget the gingerbread.

"Maggie MacLean," says the girl, once we're up the steps and into the windy salt air of the ocean. She holds out her hand and I shake it.

"Elizabeth Manteith."

"So all that's true about the castle then, is it?"

"Aye." I look about me, as we stand at the side of the deck. Beyond the shell of this vessel is only plain sea, all dark and grey and foreboding with a matching sky above. No land. No islands. Mayhaps we really are beyond Scotland already.

"Aye, Maggie," says a man, a sailor, as he walks by. She smiles a wide smile at him, before returning her attention to me.

"So were you kidnapped too?" I ask her in a whisper.

She nods. "Aye, but it's a bitty different for me. They tell us we're going to a better life? I'm already there."

I look at her in question.

"My father was no grand Laird, and no good man in any way," she says and stares out at the sea for a moment before looking round and smiling her bright smile. "But see, here I am. Every night wined and dined in the fo'c'sle, entertained by sailor's songs and dances. It's the way to do it, Elizabeth; it's the way we'll make good in the new world."

She really does look happy about it, her golden hair blowing back in the wind. Mine seems determined to wrap itself all about my face in dark tails of red.

"What is the fo'c'sle?" I ask, peeling back my hair, so I can see her properly.

"Another type of castle! It's where the crew take their victuals. Come, I'll show you."

I take her hand and we walk round the deck to the front of the ship and up some steps into the fore castle as I think it is properly called. It's no castle. But there is food. I can smell it. Meat and gravy. Maybe even vegetables. There's wine. It's put into my hand by a sailor so young he could be one of us, one of the kidnapped many. I'm not used to drinking wine, but the nearness of food after so long without, makes me gulp down half the glass at once. I'm so hungry. And so thirsty. I've had no food, except for Peter's gingerbread. And how lovely that was. Thoughts of it, and grumpy Peter himself, are somehow making me want to cry. Again. What about the others though? Did they eat while I was sleeping? How long did I sleep with my battered head? I mean, how long has this voyage been going on?

I must have spoken some of this out loud because the young sailor tells me we've been at sea for five days. And that the others are messed to eat their victuals downstairs in their quarters.

A long wooden table is being laid with food. Chicken legs. Potatoes. We don't often eat potatoes, or tatties, at home and I'm surprised to see them here. There's something green, cabbage maybe, but it's the chicken that draws me towards the plates of food. The other people in the room all find this most amusing. But I am sat at a proper table, on a proper bench and I am eating. And eating.

"Take your fill, lassie," says one man.

"Build your strength up," says another and they all laugh.

The laughter holds something of the same tone as the kidnapping guarding men, but those two are not here. These are just crew members. Innocent souls doing their work aboard a ship. It's no fault of theirs what happened to us. They don't own the boat.

The wine makes me feel so much better. But not so much better that I will sit in a man's lap. And that's what I'm asked to do. It's what Maggie is doing on the other side of table. She smiles encouragingly over to me, giving me a small nod. And, though my belly is full, I get a bad feeling there, like I've been really stupid, like I was when I walked onto the boat and got kidnapped, like I'm sinking deeper into some terrible seafaring nightmare that goes on forever and has no end but a dreadful one.

"Our wee red heid should go back wi' William first," says one of the men, causing much laughter around him. I gather that William is the really young boy, the one who could be one of us. He flushes and looks most affa unhappy.

"Aye, I think she'll be his first," says another and they all start chanting: "Willy boy, you're going to play with fire tonight!"

I slam my wine glass down and it breaks on the table. "First what?" I demand, feeling all of a sudden terribly sober.

One of the sailors speaks. He says 'first' and then he says a word so foul and so low that I will not even think it myself. But I know what it means. I've heard my cousin Matthew say it in the past when he was in one of his nastier states of mind. And now I understand why me and Maggie are being wined and dined in the fo'c'sle.

I know I'm in danger. But I am determined to get out of here in the same state that I arrived. Sometimes, when things are not as you wish them to be, you just have to behave as if they were as you wish them to be, and others fall in line with you. At least temporarily, before they think things through. It's worked in the past. I talked on and on about getting a new horse and then... well, that didn't quite work out how I planned in the end. But it should have. And this will. This has to.

I pick up the bowl of chicken and a bottle of wine like they belong to me, like I am a person who has the right to do whatever she pleases in this place. "I thank you kindly, gentlemen," I say. "But it is time for my companion and I to return to our bunks." Like we have bunks! I look over at Maggie. She has her arms around her sailor and does not look to be taking this opportunity to escape. "Maggie," I say, loud and clear.

"Oh, sit doon and drink up Elizabeth," she says, not even turning her head to look at me.

"Maybe another night," I lie. "But for tonight I bid you a good evening." And, not looking at any the one of them, I hold my head high and walk straight out of there, almost falling down the steps onto the deck, then almost falling down the steps into the hold. But almost is a big difference from actual and I am still on my feet, still standing.

Peter's sitting up, like he's been waiting for me. He stands as I approach. "Are you all right?"

"Aye," I tell him, handing him the bowl of chicken and the wine. I flush, not knowing quite what to tell him. "You were right. I shouldna have gone."

"They didna—?"

"No," I say quickly, cutting off whatever he might have been going to say.

"Sit doon, lass," he advises, and I do.

I sit down on my sack as Peter lays the food and wine on the floor and calls some of the bairns over to take it. I only lie down on my sack once Peter is back beside me.

And then I curl up in a tight ball and go to sleep.

Chapter Six

It's morning and I feel much better, even though I am lying on a sack on a wooden floor. This is the big wide world and things such as I almost came to last night are part of that big wide world. I'm not so sheltered and spoilt a wee lassie that I dinna ken this. It was a shock, is all. And now: my belly is full, or at least not as empty as it was, and I am awake, I am alive and I have a friend. A truly good friend,

I observe him now, as he sits looking around the hold, watching what's going on, smiling slightly at a game some of the bairns are playing. He's really quite handsome, so well built and strong looking. He turns his face towards me, as if sensing my study of him, and I smile into his dark eyes.

"How you doing this morning, Elizabeth?" he asks.

I sit up and sigh, glancing over at the skipping rope fun the wee ones are having. "I feel a bit older than I did yesterday," I tell him, indeed feeling much further removed in knowledge from the happily playing children now.

"Aye," he says, serious for a moment, before smiling a most mischievous smile and saying, "You still look like a bairn though."

The sheer and utter cheek of him! "I'll have you know that I am sixteen years old," I inform him.

"Really?" he says, in a completely skeptical tone, looking at me as if I am making it up.

"Aye, really," I say, giving him a playful push.

"There's no need for violence," he laughs, holding his hands up as if to protect himself from me.

Maggie, lying on her table, right against the wall or hull of the ship, stirs now, and sits up, perhaps disturbed by our banter.

"Maggie brought us marzipan!" one of the wee girls dances over and tells us, all delighted and sticky mouthed.

"Aye, ye've eaten well today," says Maggie sleepily as she turns to face our way.

She climbs down beside us and I'm not sure what to say to her. But it's Peter she speaks to anyway.

"So what do you think you'll sell for?" she asks him.

"A hundred guineas," he says, no hesitation, straight faced, looking back at her.

Maggie laughs. "I didna mean at. Who will buy you and for what purpose?"

"I'm a farmer's loon," he says. "I could work the fields."

Maggie nods. "Aye, that's probably what will happen. Tobacco's a big deal over there. That's what this ship is collecting and bringing back to Aberdeen. And what about you, Elizabeth?"

I shrug, still reticent to speak. Also, I have not given the matter any thought. I plan to escape and get home, not slave in the fields.

Maggie continues, "When they took you, and me, off the dock like they did, d'you think they were thinking: 'There goes a hardy farm worker.'?"

"No," I realise. "Housemaid? Kitchen servant?"

"That's what a lot of these wee 'uns will do to begin with," she says. "But you and me are different."

"How so?" I feel quite cross, mainly with myself because there's something here I'm not getting, like last night. Aye, this conversation has the shadow of last night upon it.

"We're nae wee bairns or hardy boys or tough wifies like the rest of them," Maggie points out. "They're looking to make a pretty penny for us from some fine gentleman with money to spare and either no wife, or a sick or ugly wife."

Still, I am slow. "So, we're to be sold as wives?"

"Well, probably nae the type that gets a ring on the finger and a fine gown. But, ye ken…" She looks me straight in the eye for this next bit. "Might be better to prepare for it."

I glare back at Maggie. I want to tell her I am no whore. For that's what's she's being, at night, there in the fo'c'sle. But I canna say it. Nae in front of Peter and the bairns. And nae to her. Apart from almost tricking me into it, she's nae doing anybody but hersel' any harm. Everybody here ate a little better because of her, and me, last night. And that's a sobering thought.

But I canna. And I winna.

And if I am bought by some fine gentleman? All the more chance to steal some money before I escape. Because yes, that I will do; I will become a thief if I have to, to survive. And to get home.

But from that day on it becomes clear that there is a huge risk to our lives here that no amount of thieving or any other crime can spare us from. Disease. It starts with the smaller children having some stomach sickness and then the wifies and some of the bigger bairns go down with it too.

Then comes the morning when one of the babies doesn't wake up. That's when Maggie stands up and stamps. She shouts at the guarding mannies as they take the tiny wee body away. She tells them we could all end up dead and what money would they make from us then?

So we get to go up on deck. I gulp in the air beside Peter, so glad of the sea spray and wind and just of the air itself.

The hold has gone completely rank. It's unbreathable down there, a stinking mess. After that first death, two more follow, another baby and a wee bairn. So we get to come up here now every day to breathe. It's nae out of kindness. I ken at. It's just as Maggie said, because we winna be worth much dead or sickly. And, of course, our reprieve disna last long. We carry the buckets up for emptying and then we take them back down with us. Into the stink.

I live for the forays up on the deck. I'm actually envious of Maggie not having to stay down with us all the night. Though I still winna go there. But I can understand how some folks might. And Maggie sometimes seems to be the happiest of us all, in her acceptance of the way things are and the purpose of this boat.

The sickness passes after a couple of weeks. Peter, Maggie and I are lucky and we don't catch it. And apart from those first few, no one else dies, which is a mercy and quite a miracle if you ask me.

One evening Maggie starts up a song and dance and gets us all laughing down there in between the cargo and the hint of sickness that still hangs in the air. We're dancing round and round, laughing and singing, and then falling asleep, as she makes her way to the front of the ship.

We're still sleepy in the morning, Peter and me, as we go up with some of the others to empty the pots and take the air. So we dinna notice that Maggie's nae there with us. She wasn't sleeping on her table or sitting up and having a wee joke and a laugh with anybody this morning.

Maggie is lying on the deck. Maggie is laid out on the deck. I see her. I know the truth of what I'm seeing but I canna believe it. This is something else I winna and canna do.

"Maggie," I say. "Get up! Fit ye dein', quine?"

There's two men there. They've got a length of cloth. They seem like they're about to wrap her in it.

I kneel down. I give Maggie a shake. To waken her up like.

She's cold. A solid weight. All the jollity and colour is gone from her bonny plump face.

I know this. I've seen it afore.

I look round at Peter, seeking his help. He's just standing there, looking grey, looking down at Maggie and then looking out to sea. I think this is something that he hasna seen afore. But he does ken what it is.

The two men start to wrap Maggie up, to roll her up in the cloth like she's a thing and not a person.

I spring back to life: "What happened to her?" I demand.

The men ignore me, as if I too am dead and voiceless.

At the far end of the deck, I catch sight of the young sailor William from the other night.

I cover the distance between us in seconds and ask him my question: "What happened to her?"

He shrugs. "I dinna ken. She wis found like that this morning."

I shut my eyes for a wee minty and take a deep breath, before asking: "Where was she found?"

"First Mate Alexander Young's bunk," he tells me, meeting my eye as he speaks, as if to tell me that First Mate Alexander Young is a bad, bad man.

Of course he is. And he has the name of a murderer if ever anyone did. I've read through many an old record in the barony court book at the castle and I know some things about crimes and what should be done about them.

"I demand to see Captain Ragg," I say.

"He's doun there," says William. "By the body."

A man has appeared there, and a right gormless glaiket fool he looks too, staring down at the roll of cloth, hands on his hips, like he's picking out a rug at market.

"She should be examined to determine the cause of death," I shout, marching towards him.

He looks at me like I'm some oddity, just there for his amusement.

"And who are you?"

"I am Elizabeth Manteith, Lady of the castle, and a kidnapped slave."

I see Peter's shoulders drop as he shakes his head at me. He's right of course. I should stop saying things like this and starting rows. But Maggie is dead and voiceless and I have a mind to lend her mine.

My own voice is silenced as a man grabs me from behind and holds his dirty great hand over my mouth. It matters not. I would have been unable to move and speak regardless. I am frozen in place, by the scene that is unfolding in front of me.

Chapter Seven

The men who rolled Maggie up in the cloth. They are lifting her. Lifting her right up off the deck. And then flinging her; they swing her back and forth a couple of times – one of them laughs – and she's hoisted over the side of the ship and into the sea. I hear the splash.

I bite the hand that's over my mouth. I bite it hard. The owner of the hand curses and lets me go and does not follow as I run to the side of the ship and look over. There's just cold swishing sea. It's not rough today. Not still either. It's never still. You wouldn't know to look at the water that anything – or anyone – had been thrown in.

I am so angry I don't know what to do. I don't know who to shout at, who to pummel with my fists.

"Dinna, Elizabeth," whispers Peter at my side, possibly divining my pummeling intentions. "It winna help her now."

"But… justice," I hiss back at him. "She should be honoured, and her killer shamed."

"You ken that's nae going to happen here."

I do. In the writings of my many greated grandmother Isobell Manteith, I read about another unjust death and how a woman performed the last rites for her friend. I remember my brother Thomas and what was done then. Maggie's body is gone, but her soul must still be flying free. So I get down on my knees, glaring at Peter to join me, which he does.

And I pray.

I don't know all the right words. But I pray out loud that Maggie's soul makes it into heaven, that she be forgiven her sins. I add some wants of my own about her killer getting what he deserves and all those that commit acts of brutality against innocent souls being dealt with too. But I come back to Maggie. I talk about how fair she was and how kind and generous.

And then I stand. And turn away from the side of the ship. And there's a fair few mannies standing there on the deck with their heads down. And some of the bairns and wifies from down below. This is Maggie's send off. This is her funeral.

I say as much to Peter when we reach the hold.

"Aye," he says. "Could have been worse. Those that are not much liked dinna have as many turn up to their funeral, or dinna get one at all. How did you ken fit to say?"

I shrug. I find now, after the shock, and the anger, there is just sadness. I don't want to speak. Or eat. I just want to sit in my corner, wrapped up in my plaid, even though it is dirty and smells only of the ship now. I spend some time trying to remember how it used to smell, how it reminded me of the castle and Eppy and Jock, but I find I canna think of them properly. I try to remember a young quine who dreamed of adventure and true love. My head won't do it. It's gone dark in there. Everything before the boat disna feel real. The accursed ship has become my whole world now.

And life on the ship? As in my head, it all goes dark. I do eat the food that Peter puts in my hand because there is a final goal still lurking someplace in my mind and I won't die because of my own neglect. But I don't see much point in anything else. Peter sits with me and tries to get me to banter, but I can't find enough words for it, nor purpose for those that do form in my mind. He puts his arm round me and says things like "C'mon, Elizabeth. This winna last forever."

I lean against him. And sleep.

Every day it smells worse, but I dinna care. This is what we breathe now and there's nae much to be done about it. Two of the wifies, an older and a younger, start visiting the fo'c'sle at night. Good luck to them. Even though they dinna bring treats back like Maggie used to.

Every day I stand on the deck of the ship with Peter and the other bairns. We go up in batches of ten or so. Livestock kept alive. Else we would be deadstock. These are the thoughts I can manage but they have no feeling to them, no real care or worry.

I don't feel anything for a long long time. It just goes on. The same. But slightly worse all the time. I stop going up on deck, despite Peter's efforts to get me to do so. I just sit here on the floor.

So I am alone sometimes. Alone in the hold. I am a thing. Like a table. Or a chair.

"I would think a nice bath would make you feel better."

It's a man. Crouching down beside me. I dinna ken him. I barely ken what a bath is anymore. Though a scene appears in my mind. A room in the castle. Eppy singing. And water that was heated over the fire. Soap that smelled of lavender. I remember these things.

The glass that the man puts in my hand smells familiar too. Or its contents do. Whisky. My father used to like it. He smelled of it sometimes. I sip the brown liquid, and then, at the man's suggestion, drink it straight down, gasping at the burning sensation it causes in my throat.

The strong drink makes me feel warm and actually quite dizzy once I'm climbing up the steps with the man and then walking out into a storm. The rain is blowing straight into my face and the wind is fierce. I need the hand that's pushing me along, else I might be blown back by the force of the weather. I'm surprised the others are still up here in this. Maybe they'll go back to the hold now.

We go round the side of the deck, the side I've not been to before, and then the wind pushes us along, my hair blowing straight out in front of me. There's rooms here. We pass a few doors, my head swimming, swimming as if I'm in the great big sea itself.

William's there, walking towards us between the rooms and the side of the deck. He wants to know where we're going and the man slaps him round the head and tells him to get gone. It's such a shock, the way the man slaps William, all of a sudden like that, for no reason. I start to feel sick. And those words: get gone. They make my head hurt. I don't want William to be hit. I don't want him to get gone. I don't want to go into this dark room with the man. There's a bunk but no bath.

"Wasn't there meant to be a bath?" I ask, the wind and the slapping and the get gone-ing having cleared my head a wee bitty, I think.

"There will be," says the man with a smile I don't like. "You can get ready for it."

With him here? I stare at him in disbelief for a moment and then he says, "I'll help ye," and grabs at the front of my dress. I'm glad for its many buttons. They dinna come loose for all his tugging at me and my pulling away from him.

And then there's more grabbing and shouting and punching, but nae of me, of the man, and it's all hands and bodies and noise and I canna deal with it, so I sit down on the floor again. Feeling what? Drunk. Stupid. I ken I've been stupid. Fo'c'sle stupid. Again.

Then I realise it's Peter who's here. And William. And they're pulling the mannie, the fo'c'sle type mannie, outside. Ootside. Outside. They're fighting with him there.

I should help. Yes. The man was bad. My mind starts to understand the fullness of that as light starts to splinter through the dark that I've sat in for so long.

So I leap to my feet and run at them, the three men, and I shove the bad one as hard as I can. He has Peter by the throat. William is trying to pull him off. But my shove changes everything. So does the wind. It helps. It pushes as well, and the side of the ship breaks. And the man goes through it, and I almost do too.

Peter has one of my arms. William has the other. And the wind screams as we all sway there, battered and blown, and shocked.

Just us three on the deck now.

No bad man.

The man has got gone. The side of the deck is gone too. I stare at the great gap in the wood, all splintered and ragged round the edges.

"Best get back down below," says William.

"Aye," agrees Peter. "C'mon, Elizabeth."

I hold Peter's hand. And we fight our way through the storm and back round to the steps and then climb back down into the hold.

Chapter Eight

I'm shaking as I sit down on the floor of the hold once again. Peter rubs my hands, and that helps a wee bit.

"I pushed him," I say. "He's dead, isn't he?"

Peter shrugs and pulls a face as if to say it doesn't matter. "Better him than you, or me. That was the room Maggie was found in, and that was Alexander Young, the man that killed her. He was trying to throw me over the side of the ship, Elizabeth. He got what he deserved."

Maggie. This ship. Bad men. What's been done to us? The hugeness and the horror of it all threatens to overwhelm me. The dark state was easier. I didn't think about any of this, or anything at all, then. And it nearly killed me.

But something else huge and dark and overwhelming soon takes over all our thoughts. As evening candlelight replaces the grey daylight that comes through the door from the deck above, the storm we experienced up on deck moves way beyond a bad bit of wind and rain. It's become a fierce gale which makes the ship tilt from side to side and the table and chairs slide about all over the place. It's so bad that people start saying we might sink.

A dark state of despair is not what will save us. I ken 'at. It's time for folks to hear some sensible words, and I think I'm the one to spik them. After all, this is just another way that we may or may not die. Drowned in the ocean when the ship sinks. It would probably be quick. But I winna say that thought to them.

Everyone is keening and sobbing, as I stand up and speak out loud and clear. "Come on noo," I tell them. "We're hardy Scottish folk. We're nae feart o' a bit of bad weather!"

"This is mair than a bit o' rain, lassie!" says a woman, and she's right of course.

The ship is making sounds like it might rip apart. Bangings and howlings like I've never heard before in my life. If the wood around us does come apart it will be an escape of sorts, an end to all this, whatever happens after.

I reach out and take Peter's hand. And we wait. Huddled together for this final scene, some of the bairns cuddled in between us too. And then we're tipped back as the great boat roars and judders around us; we fall all over the place, a heap of bodies, but living ones still. We scramble to our feet in the dark, shouting out to ask what's happened. There's no sway, no feel of the sea now, though the rage of the rain and wind continues.

"We've run aground," shouts somebody over the noise.

"Aye, I think that's it," says Peter, and, with no mannies at the door to stop us, we find our way to the ladder, and up onto the tilted deck.

"Back! Get back!" So yell our captors as we arrive beside them. They sound and look to be just as frightened as the wee bairns were down below.

"We choose who gets to come forward!" shouts one of the kidnapping mannies. "Her!" he says, pointing at one of the wifies. "And her!" He's chosen the ones who go the fo'c'sle at night.

The kidnapping mannies look at me for a moment and then look at each other. One shakes his head. The other one nods in agreement and says, "Too much trouble!"

And then there's a creaking that sounds like it's come straight out of hell itself and one of the great masts of the ship falls. We run the other way, on this no longer rocking vessel, no longer rocking but with a feeling like it's about to fall apart in the gale nonetheless.

The crew start scurrying about like rats, lanterns held aloft, and I see what they are doing. Peter sees too and he pulls us to the front of the crowd. They're lowering a boat to take us to safety. Down into the dark sea on this dark night. We must be on a sandbank or a wee island and this new craft will convey us to solid land.

Solid land. What a thought! I can't remember what it feels like to walk upon the unmoving earth, putting one sure foot in front of another. Oh, it will be grand! So I stand in the storm on the shattered ship and think of: baths, clean clothes, food, vegetables, broth, porridge, meat, new shoes, new people… a letter to my father.

"Elizabeth!" Peter is shaking me. I'd gone into a dream, but now I'm back and facing unsavoury news. The saving boat is small. The crew are all going in it and some of the wifies and some of the bairns. I see William carefully lifting some of the smaller children over the edge to safety.

"They're choosing them as will fetch more at market," shrieks a woman, and she starts up a shrill crying which carries round the wretched hull of this ship like a curse.

"It's nae for you eens," shouts one of the kidnappers. "Get doon. Back doon below." He has a whip. I've never seen a whip used on a person before, but he lashes it over us now and we shuffle back fast, gathering away from it, like a herd of frightened animals.

Soon, those of us that are to be left are below in the hold again and the hatch above is locked. The crew row away. And leave us. Like the evil cowards that they are. We are cargo, left to sink or be blown to bits when the ship finally falls apart. There is a fair amount of crying and screaming. The wee ones are feeling it the worst. I feel numb, a bit like when Maggie died, but I think morning light is starting to show through some of the cracks in the side of the ship, so we can see a wee bitty, and I can still speak. And, I can sing. There will be no punishment or trouble for the choice of song here. Most of these lowly folks probably dinna ken it onyways. Well, they can learn it now. And then they can join in.

"Oh Come All Ye Faithful," I start. "Joyful and Triumphant! Come ye, oh come ye, to Bethlehem!"

I repeat that three times to get them learning it and then walk slowly round, raising my hands. What else is there to do here? Die crying or die singing?

They join in, little by little, until mostly all of us are singing.

"Oh come let us adore him, oh come let us adore him, oh come let us adore him, Charles Edward Stuart!"

No one bats an eye. They all just sing it and it is something wondrous to behold.

The ship shudders and cracks as another mast goes. And another, the third and final one. We recognise the manner in which the hull shakes and the great noise from above. Yet, the vessel still holds together; it still keeps us sheltered from the storm.

"Sing choirs of angels, sing in exultation! Sing, all ye citizens of Heaven above! Glory to God, glory in the highest! O come, let us adore Him, Christ the Lord."

And at that, water starts to come in. This does cause a short lull in the singing but we lift the smaller ones high, up onto the wooden cargo, and we soon start up again, the water rising all around us until daylight is properly discernible through the, now larger, cracks in the walls.

I suddenly see something I hinna seen for a long while. A tree! I squint and rub my eyes before looking again to make sure, but it is! I see branches and leaves and twigs … which means: land! We can see land through the holes in the ship. And we also all notice and remark that the storm has died down.

"We have survived this night, this storm!" I say to my fellow companions. "We will have to escape our prison now and go on to live our lives as free people!"

"Aye, our captors have deserted us!" agrees Peter. "We are our own men and women noo!"

A debate starts up. We will have to break down, or up as it is, the hatch to the upper parts of the ship. Some are feart that this will lead to the ship falling apart. But we are wedged on a sandbank and near to land. We cannot remain trapped in this boat forever. We will soon starve.

A new feeling begins to grow in me. No. It's not new. But's it's been so long since I've felt it that it's strange. It's hope. Hope with some excitement mixed in. Because: what are we going to do now? In this new land? I mean, I know what I'm going to do: find the means to write to my father. But we'll have to live somewhere, eat somewhere—

"They've come back for us!" someone shouts. "We're saved!"

It's true. That they've come back anyway. I see them approach through the shattered wooden wall. The long boat that rescued the chosen few last night has returned for the remains of the cargo. For that's what we are again as we're loaded onto the smaller vessel. Peter and I look at one another, wary of what's happening now, certainly not delighted with the turn of events as most seem to be.

We're taken a short distance from what was some sort of sand bank, to an island where we stand on solid ground and look back at the hulking shell that has been our home for the last few months. What a state it is in. What a state we are in.

We camp under ragged sails, salvaged from the ship, and eat what maggoty rations were found there too. I wade into the sea, or river mouth as I can see it rightly is.

"You winna survive swimming to the mainland!" shouts one of the crew.

I ignore him. I'm not that stupid. I've come in here to get some sort of clean. My finest dress is now as brown as my poorer ones for playing in the woods at home and, grand though it once was, it is torn in places and stained and smelly. Now it smells of river. And water weeds. But not of the boat. I have said goodbye to that terrible place and thing, and it is an improvement.

We were three months on the ship called The Planter.

We are three weeks on the small island in the river of Delaware by the Cape of May.

Sailors are some use for some things. They know the names of places and where we are.

We see rain and sun and wind. We see blue skies and black clouds.

I have time to think on things. I said I widna become a whore. And I haven't. I said I might become a thief, and maybe I will. I didna expect to become a killer. I really dinna ken fit to do with that thought, that fact. It just happened. And I will have to learn to live with it.

And then: we're back in a hold, a smaller one than the last, dustier, though less smelly, and we're on our way to Philadelphia, the city of brotherly love, in this, the colony of Pennsylvania, in the new world that is America.

Chapter Nine

Peter and I huddle together on the floor of this latest prison, feeling like wild creatures left to die in a trap. We are near starved. And we are frightened. As is every one of the people here, from wee bairns to the wifies. The space is small, making our status as prisoners more obvious somehow than it was on the island or even on the original ship. There's no furniture here to help the place masquerade as living quarters. And then there's the thought of where we're headed now. We'll be there soon. We could, in fact, arrive at our destination at any moment.

The journey is smooth, stormless, and quiet too, because nobody speaks much. There's no thought of singing now. When the boat finally stops and we climb out of the hold, we are expected to walk. The energy somehow comes. I take Peter's hand and hold on tight as we travel along the quay in the grand port of Philadelphia. This is a much bigger harbour than that of Aberdeen. That is really all I can take in. I am too tired to look at all the mannies and wifies and fish, so many fish everywhere; oh mercy, I am hungry!

"Another barn," notes Peter, when we are ushered into a large ramshackle wooden building. Again we find a space to sit together, among the others. Again, we are on the floor, this time an earthen one. No chairs are provided for the likes of us anywhere now it seems. "I was kept in a barn in Aberdeen," he tells me. "Down at The Green."

I ken The Green. I used to think it was a nice place to walk through, a space between buildings, like a city version of a forest glade.

Captain Ragg struts about, excited at the thought of what monies he will soon be getting from the sale of his cargo. He looks us over and discusses us with the other men. I lean against Peter, tired of it all. He leans his head against mine, no doubt feeling the same. Our fingers are interlinked now and I study his hands, noticing how much bigger they are than mine.

Soon there are new mannies among the old, hired from hereabouts to watch over us and make sure we don't escape. Because three did. Three ran away already. But I know this is not our moment. I just ken it. And then I'm right glad I stayed when we get fed, for it is better food than I have had in such a long time. It is my wished for meal from weeks ago when I first heard we were to go on land. Meat, tatties, green vegetables. There's no gravy, but I dinna care about that. Not now. Not anymore.

Then, with our bellies full, we are to be washed. By the new mannies. No. No, no, no! I do shout this out loud. We are to be changed from our ragged clothing to look better and smell better. But the things they hold out for us quines, both small and grown, are just basic shift dresses. And there's no underwear to go with any of it.

"What I am wearing is finer than that!" I yell at our new captors.

One of them inspects me and frowns. "It's true," he says in a most proper English voice. "How did you come by such a gown?"

"I am Lady Elizabeth Manteith of the castle. I was abducted on the quayside in Aberdeen. Will you help me get word to my father?"

His frown deepens. "I cannot do that, but you can have your privacy for washing and dressing."

"And all the other lassies?"

He nods and a sheet is hung up. We are given buckets of water with soap and cloths and we all of us make the best of it. I scrub my face till it stings, and all the rest of me, and then soak and soap my hair. I put on the new dress. It is fresh and, though poorly made − Eppy would be horrified by the stitch work − it is entirely clean. I wrap my plaid round myself again but think to pin the Elfin Blade on the inside of my under garments which I am keeping on whatever they say. Some of the other women and children don't have such thick items and I feel for them as I help some of the younger quines with theirs. The thin cloth we've been given does not hide much of our bodies.

My plaid is wrenched from me by one of the mannies as soon as the privacy sheet is down and he wins the ensuing struggle.

"The buyers will think we're hiding something," is the pathetic explanation given for the theft.

"Oh, like the abduction of folk, including all these wee bairns?" I say, gesturing towards the rest of our group.

He laughs and walks off and I see him holding up my green plaid and my brown gown with the other rogues and thinking what price they could get for those too. I will not forget this. I mind most about the plaid, the one last warm comfort of home that has been taken from me.

I am in high hopes that Peter and I can escape between here and whatever place we're being sold, and I say as much to him when we are reunited after washing. He looks ruddy and scrubbed clean too and has a fresh shirt. His head has been shaved again. I have a vague memory of that happening to all the boys sometime after Maggie died.

"Aye, that would be the best," he says with a small smile, agreeing to my plan at once. "But if we canna, we must promise to find each other again, and get home, and see that these bastards get what they deserve."

"Aye." I share his determination and I grip his hand as we are marched along a street, a very long clean street, past shops and taverns, and onto: a slave block! We've had no chance to escape, being very well guarded now. We do not all go up on display at once. The slave block is just a few boards of wood held up by some barrels. They put the smaller boys up first and some get bought as a group and herded away like sheep. I am glad for them, getting to stay together like that. Hopefully that will happen for Peter and me if we keep holding hands to suggest that we are being sold as a pair of servants? There might be some house that needs a young woman and man for different tasks? But it is not to be.

As soon as we are up on the block, Peter is bought by a Scottish sounding manny and taken away. It is very hard not to bawl and cry again like I did when I was first on the ship, but I manage to stay calm. Tears run down my face though as we hug goodbye. They dampen his new shirt, thin and cheap like my shift, but he does look most affa bonny in it anyway. I touch the bit that's been made wet from my crying. I want to lean forward and kiss his cheek, but he's taken away from me before I can. He's jumping down from the slave block. He's walking away with the dastardly man that bought him. I canna believe it. I don't want it to be happening.

He turns back, the colour high in his cheeks, eyes bright and shiny, and he says "I'll see you again, Elizabeth Manteith."

"I'll find you Peter," I promise, and he nods as he's led away.

I watch them walk along the street, the mannie and Peter.

Then they go round a corner and Peter is gone.

Chapter Ten

I am alone. I have no friend from home with me now. No family. It's just me. Elizabeth Manteith of the castle. I've been spirited away across the sea, and who knows to where and what I am headed next? A wee gust of wind blows up as I stand on the boards where I've been put, and I'm surrounded by brown leaves and dust and a whirling piece of paper which I grab out of the air and glance at before hiding it in my shift. It had a name on it. A familiar name. I can't remember where I ken the name from, but it must be Scotland somewhere, and I'm keeping it. It's mine.

So the other wifies and quines are up here on the slave block with me now, and Maggie's words about what I would be sold for come back to me very clearly. Well, that canna be allowed to happen.

So I hunch my back and turn my feet in like I'm knock-kneed. And I point both my eyes to look at my nose like I am squinty-eyed. I limp as I walk up along the boards to get looked over. I cough too, for good measure.

The crowd is full of mannies, some fine, some not so fine, all rogues to be thinking of buying people as if we're things! Though some of us folks did sell our indentures in the right and legal way and these people in the crowd do not know that we were kidnapped, or how we were treated, or that we were left to die for a while in a shipwreck. So maybe they are not all bad. Not completely bad. They think of us as servants for hire, perhaps. This can be hoped for.

Captain Ragg, the man who was in charge of the ship, and no doubt all the kidnappings, buys one of the wifies who used to go to the fo'c'stle! To be a wife? The type of wife with no ring and no fine gown?

A tall man with spectacles walks over and looks me up and down. I feel sick. I try to appear sicker. What else can I do? I feign a coughing fit when he's joined by two other mannies and they wander away to look at someone else. I stand up a bit taller when a little grey haired old wifie comes over to examine me.

She asks if I can cook and clean.

"Yes, ma'am," I say, relieved to be able to let my eyes stare straight now.

"Good, good," she says.

And hurrah! She buys my indentures! Luck is with me! The old woman takes me to her cart and tells me to sit up in the back of it. There is a dark skinned woman sitting in the front, holding the reins of the horse.

"I took your advice," the old woman says to her.

"Good, good," says the woman holding the reins and she gives me a small smile.

These women seem friendly, nice even. So I waste no time in asking my most important question. "Would you help me get a letter to my father? I was kidnapped from the quay at—"

The old woman waves her hand in my face and grunts. "Enough talk, we've a drive ahead of us. We'll go home first, Sarah."

We trundle off along the straight straight streets, which are not like those of Aberdeen at all. In fact, they are rather fine. There are lush gardens by many of the large stone built houses. Lots of little red bricks everywhere in walls, not like the great granite blocks of the city back home. There's a great tall grand building. A court maybe? A place of magistrates and law makers? People I could approach with my story?

The wifie gets Sarah to stop the cart now and again so she can talk to people, and I take the opportunity to look at the paper that I caught from the wind. It's an advertisement for a play that is to be held in town, featuring the famous actor Crispin Trewelove. I have heard of him. I remember talk of him at home. My mind reaches for the information: he was in a play in London. My father went to watch it, I think. But it's his name that beguiles me. Crispin Trewelove. True love. Something stupid and silly that Elizabeth thought she might find one day. Well—

My heart beats fast. My face flushes. Of course. Though I've not put the thought together like this before: I did find him. I found my true love. I ken fine that I love Peter. I've known that for a while. And I've lost him already.

Peter. My closest companion. My dearest friend. I see his face how it looked as he was led away from the slave block, as he looked back, all sad, cheeks warm like mine now. Did he know too? Did he realise earlier than me that he was my true love?

We didna say it to each other, but that's because we're both so young and dinna ken much about these things, that's why, I muse as we trundle off again, surely growing the distance between Peter and myself. And we had plenty else to deal with without sitting down to say 'I love you' to each other. We're older now than when we first met on the floor of that dark and terrible hold though. Changed. Wiser. Things will be different when we meet again.

I stare out of the cart and see that there is a forest beyond the town and that the house we finally stop at is nearby to it.

"I need to get a few things," the old wifie says to me. "You stay here with Sarah."

"Is this your house?" I ask, thinking it very fine and sure to contain letter writing equipment and also that it probably receives many visitors that could be asked about Peter. Why, from here I would be well situated to go all around town asking after my dear friend and true love, as he is. "Should I not go inside and start work?" I ask the wifie, keen to begin my mission.

"My, you ask a lot of questions for a servant," remarks the woman. "This is my house, but your new master is a fine gentleman who lives some miles away in the countryside. We will take you there forthwith."

No, no, no. I know what being sold to a fine gentleman means, and it is not going to happen. An unfortunate scenario like that on the boat forms in my mind: me being pushed into some mannie's room, and then, driven mad by it, starting on some sort of killing spree of fine gentlemen across the country. That's not the path I choose. I hinna got time for it.

So I prepare for what I must do. My muscles clench, ready, waiting. The wifie heads for her house and I look at Sarah. She has her eyes downcast. Lowly. Humble. I wonder if she is enslaved or a paid servant? Was she bought like me? Would she like to escape too?

"I am going to run," I whisper to her. "Do you wish to join me?"

She says nothing. She keeps her eyes down. But she also does nothing to stop me or raise the alarm as I hurtle towards the forest and plunge into the trees, and run and run and run.

Chapter Eleven

Running can only go on so long, even when your body is well nourished and healthy, and mine has been starved and polluted for months now. But no one catches up with me. I soon slow to a walk and travel deeper and deeper into the forest. It reminds me a bit of the old oak wood at home, that glorious place of high trees and peace, though this place is warmer. Sun streams through the leaves above in little blasts of light and heat. It still feels like autumn though. It must be autumn at home too. There'll be apples in the orchard, and pears and plums. Oh, my belly hurts. It has been stretched out with that one good meal and now it's feeling its emptiness more desperately than it's done in a while.

I find some berries but they are not good and they make me sick. Night comes while I am sick. It is really cold. I have no plaid and no shelter and then it rains and all I can do is crouch beside a large tree and shiver, arms hugged round myself.

Day comes and I walk on. The plan is all confused in me now. Should I be heading back to the city to seek justice? Or write a letter? Where is Peter? Where am I?

I see a wee owl peering out of a hole in a tree and I do stand and stare at it for a long time. I have never seen an owl so small and so round before. So sweet. I wonder what it would taste like roasted on a spit. Like I could catch an owl when I'm this weak, with no weapon, or light a fire in this rain, with no dry tinder of any sort. I think I am going the wrong way. I know I am. I turn, fast, and find myself looking straight into the eyes of a bear. I am not imagining it. It is a huge, dark brown, fiercely furry bear. The real thing. A proper bear.

I stand still on my two legs and stare at it. It stands still on its four legs and stares at me. I do not wonder what it would taste like roasted on a spit. It has a wee nick missing from its ear, like a dog gets when it's been fighting with something. And then – I dinna mean to – I sneeze.

The bear rears up and stands on its hind legs. It tilts its head back and roars, real loud like, the sound resounding all round the forest. It's waving its arms about. I see its long black claws and then everything starts to sway and spin and – oh no – I'm dizzy, like I'm about to pass out. I ken it. The sheer and utter frustration of it! To come all this way, to survive all manner of evils, just to be eaten by a bear! I turn to attempt an escape before I faint, and a branch catches me across the face, and then the world goes black.

When I come to, it is warm and dry and there is the smell of smoke and food and there is no bear, only two people leaning over and looking at me, one of them fiddling with my head.

"No!" I shout and try to scramble back, only to be unable to move, being all weak and stupid and dizzy.

One of the people holds up their hands as if to calm me. "It's all right, lady," she says. "You're safe with us."

My eyes are clearing of sleep and I can see them better now. "Oh, you're just twa quines," I say.

"Twa quines?" the nearest quine repeats, sounding out the words, clearly not understanding the meaning.

"Two lassies, girls," I explain, trying to sit up and managing this time, but oh my, does my head hurt!

"That's what we are, all right," says the nearest girl with a small smile. "Three girls now, with you. I was just treating your head, miss. It's taken a bit of a bashing. Would you be fancying a bit to eat this morning?"

Would I? I nod, so hungry there doesn't seem to be words for how much I want something to eat, and I am handed a steaming bowl. Broth. There's meat in it. And some sort of vegetable. It tastes strange to me but, oh, so good. I tell the girls so and they smile, or I think they do, there is little room in me for attention to anything but the broth. I feel myself coming to life as I eat, gaining strength and vitality again.

When I'm finished, I realise that both quines have just sat and watched me eat and that maybe I did gobble up the food like a wild animal. "Thank you so very very much," I tell them.

The quieter girl comes near and kneels down to hand me a wooden cup containing some sort of tea. Now, I don't know these people, but somehow I know I am safe, to drink this, and to be with them. These quines both have kind eyes. There's nothing sneakit about them. Nothing threatening. And if I'm wrong, what's the worst that could happen? Kidnapping? Transportation to another land to be sold as a slave? I choke a wee bitty on the tea at the thought.

I drink the hot liquid down and feel better yet. And there's more. I'm given a wee cake thing. It's purple and chewy and a little bit sweet. It's nice. It's filling me up to the brim.

"That's American travelling bread," says the first girl, who has dark skin like the woman Sarah, from the cart, and the house in town. "Made with what people call Indian corn. Hannah's an American. What white folks call Red Indians."

"It's lovely," I say. "As good as any Scottish bannock."

"Is that where you're from? Scotland?" Still, only the one girl speaks.

"Aye," I tell them both. "Kidnapped on the quay in Aberdeen, transported here, sold to a wifie who was going to give me to a man, and so I ran away." The whole sorry tale is told in one sentence, one breath.

"We both escaped men too," the same quine tells me. "What's your name, girl?"

"Elizabeth—" I start and they both laugh.

"That's my name too!" says the talkative girl. "But I's called Eliza mostly. So we can share the name. You take the other part of it and be Beth! And this is Hannah. She doesn't have much English yet, but she's learning. She understands more than she can say."

All right. I can be Beth. Here in the woods. In Pennsylvania. In America. Far from home. With these quines.

"Come sit by the fire, Beth," says Eliza, and I do.

Eliza tells her tale. She was born a slave, her mother having been snatched off the beach in Africa when she herself was but a wee quine. When Eliza was considered grown, the master took her into the house with him, away from the slaves' quarters, and what happened there led her to this life in the woods. There she met in with Hannah, who was not enslaved, but was sorely treated by one of her own kinsfolk, and they live here in the forest and get by very well together.

"Len-ap-ay," says Hannah, the first word she has spoken to me. She lays her hand on her heart as she says it.

Eliza explains: "Hannah is of the Lenape people, a tribe that you folks calls Delaware after a white man who came here." She pauses. "So tell us, Beth, do you ever see the likes of us in Scotland?"

"Quines? Aye, of course."

"Black folks. Negroes. Injuns."

"Oh," I say and think. "No. Not in Scotland, and I have never met a Lenape." I try to say the name correctly and Hannah smiles. "But in London, many years ago, I did meet a black man and he was a fine gentleman. My father knew him."

"Your father is a fine gentleman too?"

I nod, saddened by the new meaning the term has come to take on for me. "I have to get word to him about what has happened to me. I have to write him a letter."

"You can read and write, Beth?"

"Aye," I say, not entirely disliking my new name. It sounds softer than Elizabeth, kinder somehow. "But where to find the means to send a letter? And to start to search for Peter? From the boat, he's my... friend." I feel shy about telling people that Peter is my true love. It is my own secret, deep in my heart. For now.

The two quines look at each other and smile.

Chapter Twelve

"Tell me again where we're going?" I ask, having helped with the packing up of camp without much information coming my way.

"Do not worry," says Eliza. "He will most likely not be there."

"He, being?"

"Mr Lay. He wrote a book all about how folks should not keep slaves. It did rile up the Quakers."

I lift my share of the burden of food and cooking equipment. In truth it is not much; they travel light, these lassies. And I have nothing at all of my own, other than the clothes I am wearing. I notice that Eliza is wearing a shift, similar to mine, but with layers of other clothing underneath. Hannah has soft leather clothes, also layered like Eliza's.

"What are the Quakers?" I ask. Like a wee bairn, every bit of information I am given leads to a new question.

I learn that Quakers are religious folk that quiver when the holy spirit is upon them. And that this Mr Lay we are to visit is one of them. But he does not keep slaves and some of the Quakers do. He also does not eat or wear anything that has come from slavery, human or animal. This sounds strange to me and I'm not sure I understand.

"He grew all his own food when he lived there, at the cave, and much of it is still growing yet. We can take all we need; he told us that before."

I have so many questions that they pop out of my mouth in quick succession: "He lives in a cave? How can that have writing equipment? And, what food?" My belly is still grumbling a wee bitty.

Soon I know that it is not actually a cave but a cottage built to look like one. The more the quines tell me, the more I feel like I am walking towards a great tale of enchantment, or perhaps I'm already in one, one with a very dark beginning. Hopefully there is a happier ending to come, one where I reunite with my true love and go home.

So we tramp through the forest and I can't help but think how much Prince Charles would like it here with all the birds and different creatures there might be to chase, and then that thought leads to how or where he is now, and then onto Eppy and Jock, and then to guilt that Eppy and Jock came last in my thoughts.

Hannah touches my arm and her face is full of concern. Has she discerned my thoughts somehow? The strangeness of everything around me is leading me to fanciful thinkings indeed.

"Tell me more about Mr Lay," I say because he sounds a peculiar character, living in his cave cottage, as he does, or did, and I should be more prepared for the meeting. The stories the girls tell me grow so outlandish that I wonder if they are teasing me. It is both of them that tell me now; Eliza translates what Hannah says in her own melodious language which makes me think of the Gaelic.

Mr Lay did stand out in the snow in his bare feet and stab a bible that was filled with some red juice to look like blood. He did this in front of the congregation as a message about slavery.

Mr Lay is friends with important gentlemen from Philadelphia; the governor of the land once dined with him in his cave.

Mr Lay did once kidnap a fellow Quaker's son to show him how it felt to lose your child like that to slavers. People from Africa are most often taken and transported here against their will.

I don't like that Mr Lay did kidnapping and say so.

"Twas only for a day," Eliza tells me. "The boy had as much fun at the cave as he did at home most likely!"

But most importantly of all: Mr Lay, having written a book, will most definitely be sure to have left writing equipment in his old home – he moved from it some years ago with his wife, but he still visits – and I can at least get a letter written to my father.

We walk for most of the day, past trees far taller than any I have seen before, some as wide as small houses. Past streams and rocks. Down paths little trod, except by animals and us quines.

Evening is falling when we reach our destination. We smell smoke and Hannah goes round the back of the dwelling to investigate, while Eliza and myself stay hidden in the trees. Hannah blends in well with the forest in her leather clothing; she is all but invisible. And the cave looks like a natural part of the place too, being covered in green growing things. For a moment the world takes on a dizzying unreality, as if none of this is actually happening, all is pretend and hidden and I am but in a dream.

But then Hannah is coming toward us in the dim light and I see that a door has opened behind her in the strange little house and that a strange little figure has appeared there.

The quines' stories have not prepared me for the person that is Benjamin Lay. He comes forward and takes our hands in greeting, one quine at a time, before ushering us into his home where I do immediately feel most welcome.

Mr Lay is very short, shorter than I am used to seeing a grown man be, and I am used to many people being shorter than me, myself having been compared to a tree too many times to mention. But he is hardly up to my chest. His own chest is wide and barrelled and his back hunched, and his legs so skinny they hardly look up to the challenge of bearing the weight of his body. His eyes are kind, his smile hidden in a very large beard.

We are soon sat beside the fire with nuts and berries and bread, and it is a very fine meal in a very fine house. That is the true reality, whatever other so called 'fine folks' might think or see.

I tell Mr Lay my tale and he promises to aid me in writing a letter in the morning and to think about how to best go about finding Peter. He does question us about odd details that seem to matter little to me in the flickering firelight of the cottage. The wifie who bought me, he is most interested in her, and Sarah her servant, and the look of the house. I can hardly remember. I was only intent on escaping it. But aye, it was painted blue with cream shutters. I do remember that, now that he asks.

Mr Lay nods and says he will think of how best to help me, and that us girls can have the bed for the night. I have a strange moment of unreality again as I look at the bed in delight. It is quite small with a coarse type of blanket upon it, but there is plenty room for us three slim quines. We will be cosy in there together. We will be snuggled and warm like wee kittens in a bed. Elizabeth Manteith of the castle, so bored, so spoilt, would have been horrified by this sleeping arrangement. She would have said 'sheer and utter' things about it. But Beth, who slept for months on the hard wooden boards of a stinking hold and then passed out on the forest floor? To her, this is bliss; this is luxury.

The ceiling above us is wild and natural like the forest. I am safe and with friends and all is well.

Chapter Thirteen

"Wake up Beth, wake up!" It is Eliza. And Hannah. And they are most affa excited for me to go somewhere with them. Mr Lay is preparing breakfast over his fire, and we are to go and clean ourselves first. Just us quines. Mr Lay does not come with us. There is no feel of the fo'c'sle here.

So we're running through the forest, like I did when I first entered the place, but also not like it at all, for this is joyful. For a short while I can forget all my woes and goals and just be running! The sun is newly up and we are skipping and dancing between the trees, our faces showing bright now and again as the sunlight catches us through the leaves.

We come to a lake, a wee lake, not unlike the wee loch by the castle. And I do love it. It feels so long since I have stood and stared and just looked at beauty. In Scotland, I looked and I did not see. Well, I see now. And we're going in. Right down to our underclothes. No! Right down to nothing at all! I stop, shocked by the quines' disrobing.

"It is only us here," Eliza assures me, standing there wearing nothing at all in the dappled sunlight. "Only us quines, as you say, Beth! And we're all made much the same!"

Well, that is obviously true. Eliza and Hannah have all the same parts as I do. And don't us Manteiths have a history of bathing in the wild? Isn't that how my mermaid grandmother met my grandfather, who she thought was a bear when she saw him? I dispense with my clothes and step into the cool water, and then submerge and swim. I haven't swum since I was a wee lassie! It feels so good, so freeing, like flying. As if I was a fairy or a sprite or a bird. Aye, or a mermaid.

I stop in the middle of the pool and let the quines catch up, and then I tell them the tale of the mermaid and the bear, and they love it. They laugh and clap their hands. And they tell me that there are real bears around these parts. I go to tell them of the one I met but then I stop, not being sure if that was a dream or not. If it had been real, would the animal not have eaten me up? Or at least injured me in some way? It all seems unreal, again like I am in a magical story from a book of strange creatures and people and places. And it does make me a wee bit quiet for a moment.

We squeeze our damp bodies into our clothes and run back through the trees to the smell of… porridge! It is slightly different than I am used to, but porridge all the same.

"Oh, Mr Lay, this is mighty good," I tell him, from my place on the floor, cross legged in front of the fire. The porridge is made with Indian corn which is much sweeter than oats. He has put berries through it and they are little bursts of sour on my tongue, but lovely.

There on the desk is paper, pen, ink and sealing wax. Tears come to my eyes. I can write to my father. But, now that the much wished for moment has finally arrived, what to say? Mr Lay gives me an address to put in the letter, somewhere my father can get word to me. I don't recognise it, but I put it down nonetheless and then I write out my long tale of woe.

I say it was not Jock's fault. I apologise for being so foolhardy. And then I pause. For what will my father do? What will he think and feel about this? A shudder of doubt appears for the first time, just for a second, but it's there. Most of the monies that used to pay for servants and fine things in the castle are now directed towards the Jacobite cause. Will my parent even want to pay for me to be returned to him? Me, whom he now sees but one or two times a year? I brush the thought aside; this is a letter that must be written and must be sent. I make sure to write about Peter too and his kindness to me on the ship. Again, I don't mention that he is my true love. My father does not need to know that at this point. In fact, maybe it is better that he does not. He might not approve, nor understand, until he has met Peter himself.

Mr Lay tells me he will see that the letter is sent. He is heading back to Philadelphia. As am I.

"What?"

"Sometimes God puts people on a path for a purpose," he says. "And you were bought by a Quaker woman that is known to me."

I bristle like a spiny brush. "Aye, as a gift for a fine gentleman."

"She can't go back there," says Eliza, also spiky and bristling. "We all know what slave owners do to young girls, young quines. We don't want any of that to happen to Beth."

"You were bought to cook food for a crippled man," Mr Lay tells me. "More crippled than me," he adds with a laugh. "He has one servant, the brother of Sarah who you did meet, and they live out of town on a tobacco plantation. The master never leaves his room. I am guessing that Mrs Sauer chose you to bring a bit of womanly order back into the house."

"Well," I say, angry, "I don't want to bring womanly order anywhere. I'm happy living in the forest with the quines until such time as I can be returned to Scotland. And I have to find Peter, so he can go home along with me."

Mr Lay nods. "We are all going to ask after Peter and see if we can find out where he was taken."

"But you would have me return to the life of a slave?"

"Michael is not like Mrs Sauer," says Mr Lay. "He does not own slaves. He freed his manservant who now chooses to stay in employment with him. I suspect the same fate lies ahead of you. Do you really want to live in the woods in winter? These two are made of tougher stuff than a fine lady from a castle."

Maybe I should stop telling everyone that is what I am, because: "I am tough. Scottish winters are fierce! And the castle is nae really a very cosy place, ye ken?"

"Letters can reach you more easily at a house with an address," counters Mr Lay. "You could write more of them from there with no difficulty. As many as you like, I should think."

"Well… I can write them here." But his arguments are sinking in. Scottish winters are fierce, yes, and that means I can imagine how cold it might be here in winter. In the woods. Under the giant snow covered trees. I am in fact frightened for the quines, but they assure me they can go to Hannah's people if it gets too bad. There are those who would be safe for them to stay with, but those people might not want a total stranger, such as I am, staying with them.

In the end we reach a compromise. I will go with Mr Lay to Philadelphia, back to the horrid old woman who purchased me from the slave block as if I was an object in a shop. But if I do not like it there I will return here and make a new plan. The quines will be nearby at the beginning of this 'path' as Mr Lay keeps calling it. And so will he.

Chapter Fourteen

So here I stand. On the doorstep of the wifie, the buyer of young girls, waiting to see if she or Sarah will answer the door. Mr Lay stands to my right and — I look round to the left and into the trees to check — aye, I catch a wee glimpse of movement: the quines are there.

I fiddle with my new bracelet, my beautifully plaited leather finery. Hannah gave it to me and I have never owned anything quite like it. I gave her the silvery Elfin Blade, but with a warning that it possibly does not bestow good luck as it is meant to. She is going to bless it and then some time in the future when we meet again we are to swap our friendship gifts back. Touching the leather is comforting and I grip it tightly as the door opens.

It is Sarah who opens the door to us. She's older than I realised previously, with greying hair and lines round her eyes. She curtseys to Mr Lay and I think I see the flash of a smile when she looks at me, but I could be wrong; it's over so fast. She invites us inside. I give a quick look back to the trees, and then I step over the threshold and into my new life.

We sit in what seems to be a parlour to wait for the horrid woman Mrs Sour.

"Sour? It suits her," I whisper to Mr Lay who then explains that the name is Sauer, not Sour, and that the family originate from Germany.

She arrives and looks most put out to see me. As advised by Mr Lay, I do not speak, but I think many unkind thoughts about Mrs Sour, who is still sour to me. She is wrinkled and pointy-nosed and mean, and she narrows her eyes at me.

"Well, well, Betty Mackay, come back I see. And there was I about to put notices round town."

I want to speak so much. It's too much. I have to speak. "I am Lady Elizabeth Manteith of the castle."

Mrs Sour raises a sceptical eyebrow but says nothing.

"It's to Michael she's to go?" asks Mr Lay.

Sour nods. "To Michael's house. We shall away this minute. Sarah! Sarah!"

I flinch. Sour has a bellow of a shout on her. A bit like the first whine of a bagpipe before the tune gets going. Poor Sarah scurries in and is instructed to get the cart ready for the trip to Michael's house. I can tell Sarah is pleased by this. Of course. She will get to visit with her brother.

"There's no need for us to detain you any longer, Mr Lay," says Mrs Sour and I understand this to mean: 'Leave immediately; I do not like you and I think you beneath me.'

"I'll be keeping an eye on young Elizabeth," says Mr Lay, standing to leave.

"There's no need for that," replies Mrs Sour. "She'll be well occupied in her new position."

I stand too. And hug Mr Lay. Which makes everyone uncomfortable, I think.

"I will make sure your letter is sent safely," he says, stepping out of my hug. "I am taking it to my good friend Mr Franklin. He will get it onto the right ship. You should visit his printing shop in town, Elizabeth; he sells books and pencils and good chocolate there."

When Mr Lay goes, I do feel rather lost and alone in this strange and unfriendly family. Mrs Sour instructs Sarah to, "Get her ready, get her ready!" and through we go to a back room, Sarah and I. There, I change into a dark blue gown. It's very plain and clearly that of a servant, but it is the finest thing I've worn since I set foot on this continent, my own old dress having been dirtied and damaged during capture and voyage, and the new shift being just a thin and cheap package in which to be sold.

So I think about gowns. Sarah looks me up and down and fetches a kerchief for me. I tuck it in round my chest, feeling quite pleased with it, not that my new garment is particularly revealing but a kerchief is a truly grown up thing to be wearing. I like the look of it and I feel properly dressed and civilised again, in a way I haven't felt since Scotland. I thank Sarah who rewards me with that quick and then gone again smile.

I think of the castle and how empty it has felt since Thomas died and my father took to travelling and all the servants were let go. Almost all the servants. Not Jock. Not Eppy. How does it feel there, to them, with me gone too?

"You do look most proper, miss," says Sarah.

"Does your brother like working for Michael?" I ask.

She looks surprised and the smile lasts a little longer this time. "They are real close," she tells me. "The two of them will leave you be to do what you likes there, I'm thinking."

The bagpipe bellow that is Mrs Sour's voice sounds and we're off, Sarah driving the horse like before, Mrs Sour sitting up front, and me in the back like the luggage. Like? I *am* the luggage. The goods to be delivered, and I wonder about darting into the trees again. It would be so easy. The quines are near, I ken it. I could change my mind. But I don't. I can feel a nip in the air. It brings to mind the later parts of autumn, and the lighting of fires, and making of broth, and the laying of warm blankets upon the beds. If I am really to get a house to do with as I see fit, I will do all these things soon. And if not? If I am ordered about or treated cruelly, I will run into the trees. Or through the tobacco fields as may be the case where we're going.

It is a long way from one house to another, not the distance of the castle to Aberdeen, much shorter than that, but it still takes a while. We soon leave the grand red brick buildings and houses and gardens of Philadelphia and travel out into the countryside. The forest remains close and it is a comfort. After a time we pass along a lengthy track with the giant trees on one side and big leafy plants that I assume are tobacco on the other. There are many workers out there in among it. Lots of black faces, some white. I wonder how many of them sold their indentures in the correct and legal way and how many were just taken.

And then we're arrived and there's a stilling of the air like happens in the stone circle back home sometimes, a quiet pause in time, as I look at the house. It is very like Mrs Sour's own house but the paint is peeling all over the place and the windows are dirty. The ground around the house is dusty too, and then a little further out is rough ground, all full of spindly dead weeds. No one cares for this place. It's all hung about with neglect.

No one comes out to greet us. And no one knocks. Sarah holds the door open for Mrs Sour and me, and in we go.

Chapter Fifteen

Mrs Sour stands in the small entrance hall and shouts. "Michael! Michael!"

We hear movement above. I look at Sarah and this time I can tell that her smile is meant to encourage me to be brave and not run straight into the trees. We all stand and listen to the footsteps. They are slow. Coming down the stairs, I think. Thud, thunk. Thud, thunk.

Finally a man appears and I take it to be Sarah's brother, him looking quite like her, though older, I believe, much older. He is bent and slow with age. His smile is slower too, not as quickly hidden, but tucked away it is, as he looks at Mrs Sour.

"Is he awake?" demands Mrs Sour without so much as a 'hello' or a 'good afternoon'.

The man nods and Mrs Sour tells us all to wait in the kitchen, before setting off up the stairs herself. Her footsteps are quick and stern; they reach their destination soon and stop.

The man eyes me uncertainly as we walk through into a big airy kitchen, so much lighter than its counterpart in the castle, but so much dirtier. The floor is unswept, the table unscrubbed; there's a stale looking half loaf of bread and some cheese that's all curled-up round the edges on a plate.

"She's all right, this one," says Sarah to the man, tilting her head towards me. "She ran away, then come back. After inviting me to go with her." And then she laughs and hugs her brother.

I ignore them as much as I can, to let them have their visit together and continue my inspection of the room. Big, big, grimy windows overlook the large patch of weeds. There's a big, big fireplace made of the same red colour bricks as those grand houses in Philadelphia and it has a built in oven with wee wooden doors. I open the doors and peer in. It's dusty, not been used in forever, but it would be a fine place to make some fresh bread.

There's a loud bang and we all look at each other. It came from above, and is quickly followed by shouting.

Sarah's visit with her brother seems to be over. He makes his slow way out of the room and back up the stairs, his footsteps drowned out by the shouting.

It is Mrs Sour and, presumably, Michael that are making the din. Sarah and I follow her brother to the foot of the stairs and listen to the noise from above. The shouting is all about me. It seems I am not wanted here. I catch the words, "No more slaves," from the male voice and then Mrs Sour shrieking about the state of the place and something about a father and a mother and... I don't know what, because I retreat back into the kitchen.

Because what are my choices? The trees and the quines? Aye, that's a fine choice, filled with freedom and happiness, though the cold does worry me a bit... quite a bit actually, and here, once Mrs Sour is gone back to her own house, I could probably do whatever I wish. I could certainly write letters every day. I could get up real early to do it, or write at night if I had to. I could clean up this room; in fact, that is an excellent idea. I find a brush and sweep the floor. Sarah, having likewise re-entered the kitchen, watches me as I clean. I make fast work of the first task I have set myself. I ken I have to be fast.

"You sit doon and take the weight off your feet for a bit," I tell Sarah, pointing at the chairs which are tucked under the table. She's not as old as her brother but she's not young either and I can see that she has to do a fair bit of running about for Mrs Sour.

She pulls out a chair.

"Wait," I say, having seen the thick layer of dust upon the seat. There's a jug of water and a cloth and soon the chairs are shiny clean and Sarah sits doon.

I find salt, and the table is soon scrubbed. Then I sit doon too and look at Sarah. She seems nice. Easy enough to talk to, so I ask her a most pressing question.

"Would you know how to find out where folks that was sold at the slave block went after? Where they ended up, like?"

Sarah frowns, perhaps a bit confused by the question.

So I explain. "My friend, Peter… Peter Williamson; he was sold the same time I was. And I need to find him."

Sarah looks back at me, nodding, thinking.

And in case she doesn't realise how important a matter this is, I cast embarrassment aside, and tell her: "He's my true love."

This gets a response: a quickly tucked away laugh. Or maybe not tucked away. It's more like she found it funny, but then, all of a sudden, she didn't.

"I will tell Mrs. Sauer to ask every person we knows about this young man," says Sarah.

"Really? You can tell her to do things?"

"Oh yes," she says with a smile that does not get tucked away. "When something is important enough, I have my say and she listens."

"And you'll send word to me here if you find anything out?"

Sarah nods. And I know I have to stay now. I have to have a base where I can be reached. Mr Lay was right about that. And a clean kitchen might not be enough to secure my place here. Mannies don't often care much about that sort of thing. And the shouting from upstairs has not abated any, so it may be that I am still not wanted.

I look in the pantry. In truth it is all but bare, but I find flour and fat and an onion. I hold the onion in my hand and stare down at it for a wee minty, feeling all mixed up and strange. The last time I held an onion was in Scotland. It was part of the last meal I ever prepared there. This is the first time I've held an onion in America. They're pretty much the same here or there, so I dinna ken why I'm feeling so odd, but the onion feels important, like it's a link to home. And then I decide it's going to be a part of the first meal I ever prepare here.

The tall weeds outside are so dry that they make excellent kindling. I find firewood in the back of the pantry and now my wee oven is lit.

I smile at Sarah who is looking at me as if I am providing some sort of theatrical entertainment.

"I want to stay," I explain. "And it sounds as if I might not get to."

We both look up at the ceiling, above which the argument continues.

"It is oftentimes like this," she tells me. "Could go on till it is dark. You've made the kitchen your own already, Miss Elizabeth," she says, looking round. "Strange for a fine lady from a castle."

"I stayed in the kitchen with the housekeeper and Greeve much of the time," I explain. "After my brother died. I learned to cook and clean."

Sarah nods, accepting my tale for the truth that it is. "And what is this you're making now?" she asks.

"An onion tart." It is the perfect dish for me to bake. Basic ingredients make for quick work, and the onion smell will carry all the way up the stairs of this household that I am sure has not seen or smelled proper cooking for a long while. I'm hoping it earns me my position. Men, even shouty angry men, like their food. It is sad that I have no other vegetables or meat but this will have to do. I make two tarts. Sarah insists on helping with the pastry and she hums as she does it. I soon join in, inventing my own words for the melody; we are a noise-some household indeed.

The tarts are ready. I leave one near the open oven door to stay warm, propped up on a stool, and I cut slices for Sarah and I. Whatever the outcome of the shouting today, we shall have full bellies this afternoon.

Silence descends from above as we finish our meal. I found good plates in a beautiful closet in another room. They were not even dusty. I have a pile of them sitting beside the second tart.

Sarah and I both stand as Mrs Sour's feet, quick and stern, are heard upon the stairs.

"Sarah," she says, looking into the room.

Sarah squeezes my hand before following Mrs Sour out of the house. I watch from the front door as they climb into the cart and ride away. Mrs Sour said nothing to me. Am I to stay? Has the man, Michael, accepted me? Or am I rejected, and just left to run off and do as I will? Surely not. I think the mean old woman would want her money back; she would probably attempt to resell me if this were the case.

"That's a mighty fine smell," says a man's voice from behind and I turn, half excited, half afraid, to see my new master, a strange long lost feeling of lightness and tickliness in my belly. But it is the old man from before who stands there, Sarah's brother. I did not hear his feet this time.

"It's onion tart," I say and walk back through to the kitchen.

Chapter Sixteen

As I hoped, the man follows me, interested to see the food that has been made.

"Will you take a piece?" I say, gesturing towards the second pie by the oven. "You could sit here at the table and I could take some up for the master." That would be a good first introduction, bearing food in front of me.

The man is shaking his head, back and forth continually. "Tis only me that goes upstairs," he says with a firmness that does rile me up a bit.

"But I am here now," I say, "and I can skip up those steps much quicker than you, old man."

Now, this does rile him up a bit. His head shaking becomes faster.

"The master is not a well man. He won't see anyone but me."

"And who are you?"

"I am Comfort," he says.

"Comfort? Is that a real name?" I am now deliberately riling this poor old man and I'm not even quite sure why.

"I was my mamma's Comfort after she came off the slave ship. She had me the same day she arrive."

"I arrived as a slave too," I tell him, softening. "I was kidnapped in Scotland and brought here. Mrs Sour purchased me at the market."

He shakes his head again. "She bought your indentures, not you. And indentures don't last forever. Was you chained on the ship?"

It is my turn to shake my head.

"Was you locked down below all the time?" he asks.

"I got up on deck. Once a day. We all did."

"Did many die?"

"A few."

"I was given the same brand as my mother," he tells me, pulling up his sleeve and showing me a strange curling scar which, along with the rest of what he has said, brings it home to me that there are experiences far worse than mine. "Let me see how it goes with Michael now," he says, eyeing the tart as he pulls his sleeve back down.

I use a knife to share the tart out onto two of the fine plates. Comfort shows me where the ale is kept down low in the pantry where I had not noticed it, and then he makes his slow way up the stairs with a tray. And he stays there for a most affa long time.

I wander through the downstairs of the house, exploring, stopping to closely examine the fine room that contains the china closet. It also contains many other pieces of furniture of interest. Two small tables, more chairs like those in the kitchen and, most interesting of all, a Dutch box bed. I've seen one of these before when I was very young but I can't remember exactly where. And I want it for myself.

It has not been slept in for some time; it is slightly musty, but not damp, not dirty. Further exploration of the downstairs reveals a parlour, more cupboards and closets and fresh – well, as fresh as possible – bed linen. My bed is made by the time Comfort makes his thunking thudding way down the stairs.

I meet him in the kitchen. "I give it to you, Miss," he says. "That's the best meal we've eaten in a long long time. But I'm to tell you that you are free. You can go."

For some reason my heart sinks at this; I mean, I've cleaned and cooked and made my bed and everything.

"You can stay on as cook, if you want," he adds. "You will be like me. You will have a wage."

"That will suit me well for just now," I say, relieved, and hold out my hand to him. I'm about to introduce myself as Lady Elizabeth Manteith of the castle, but then I don't. I'm here now. In America. And I am: "Beth."

He takes my hand and shakes it, which makes me want to cry. It feels like something momentous has just happened, and also a little like I've just betrayed my home and my country and my family by using my new name, and I need to be cross and bossy.

So I tell Comfort about the disgrace of the pantry, how shockingly empty it is. And he tells me they get provisions delivered each morning from the cook house of the plantation. It seems the inhabitants of this house have been living mainly on bread and cheese. This information riles me up worse than before even. One of these men is old and stiff, and one is crippled and ill. They need proper nourishment!

"Well, this canna go on," I tell him. "I will go to this cook house and arrange better food. And I will prepare it fresh here each day. And I will need wood for the fire and more water than this jugful? What about milk? And meat?"

"You will need to speak to the foreman about all that," says Comfort, looking closely at me, something strange in his voice. And then he bends forwards and laughs. He draws breath and laughs some more. It seems he cannot stop laughing. At last he leans on the table, shaking his head free of the hilarity.

"I'm sorry, girl. I'm sorry. I is not laughing at you." He laughs again. "But you are going to set a fire under all these folks here. I can see it. And I'm thinking Mrs Sauer does not know what she's put in among us this day. And that she might not much like it if she did."

I'm not sure what to think of this. But I am sure of one thing. I am tired. And I have made my bed. And it is time for me to lie down in it. Comfort tells me he sleeps upstairs; he is unperturbed by my laying claim to the fine bed, though I suspect he wants to laugh when I tell him about it.

I listen to him walk up the stairs and remember Eppy giving something to Jock for his stiff joints. Some sort of tea. And what actual condition is the Master afflicted with? Maybe similar to Comfort, complaints of old age. I can do some good here before I go home, I am sure of it. Tomorrow I will explore the plantation and the cook house, and down in the near parts of the forest, and see if there's any sign of the quines.

But for now, climbing into my new box bed and closing its curtains, I thank God for saving me from the worst things that could have happened, thinking of Maggie and Comfort and his mamma, and the wee boys that were herded away like sheep, and Peter. Of course, Peter. Where is he now? Is he in some similarly cosy comfy warm bed? I do hope so. I pull out the paper with *Trewelove* written on it, hug it to my chest, and fall asleep.

Chapter Seventeen

The house has that 'everyone sleeping' atmosphere to it this morning. I ken I am the only soul awake here. I can feel the spirit of the home better like this as I pad through the rooms in my stockinged feet. Really it is quite a peaceful place. I open the front door and breathe in the smell of the nearby forest. It's fresh. And like home. And full of that first chill of autumn; the low sun is coming through the trees and making shadows across the porch. I walk back through the house and open the back door, and discover that the scent of the air is slightly different. There on the step is a basket containing a loaf of bread and a large wedge of cheese and a keg of ale. My first planned task is to improve upon what is left here each day, but I take the provisions inside and lay them on the table.

And then I return to the door and the air there, because there is something familiar, something that tugs at a memory, but not one from Scotland. It's smoke, a very particular smoke made from very particular sticks, I am sure. It's only a hint, it's not very close, but, shoes quickly found, I run past the patch of high weeds and down into the trees, following my nose.

I move quietly through the forest, being real careful with my feet like the quines are, in case I am wrong. But I am not wrong. It is them. And it is so good to see them. After hugs and smiles and assurances of wellbeing from us all, I sit at the fire with the quines and eat mushrooms and wee fishes as I tell of all that has happened.

"Those slaves," says Eliza, after hearing my tale, "Comfort and Sarah. I heard they was brought up from Virginia when they was young. They bin in that family a long long time."

"Sarah's a good person," I tell them. "She's going to make Mrs Sour ask all around about Peter. And Comfort is all right too, I think. He's very old. All sore and stiff. I mind on Eppy making some tea for a similar affliction that Jock had. But their food canna be helping any." I tell them of the bread and cheese and ale, and then realise I'd better return before my absence is noticed, though what anyone would do, I don't know. I am free again. Not that I ever appreciated it before. And that makes me sad. I was so ungrateful back in Scotland. I kind of knew it about myself, but not how I understand it now.

The quines walk some of the way through the trees with me, insisting I take mushrooms and some of the little fishes back to the house. Where will I say I got them, I wonder? For though it has never been explicitly spoken, I know the quines cannot risk being seen, or known about, or, in fact, captured. They are wanted women. Or girls hiding from bad things, and I mustn't jeopardise them in any way. But in the end, nobody asks where I got the food.

I light a small fire in the main fireplace and put the, now cold, fish and mushroom breakfast in a big pot I find down in the corner. It is a Dutch oven. Once more with the Dutch. Aren't these people supposed to be German? As the contents get hotter, I remove the lid and give it all a stir. The scent rises and it is not long before the thunk thud of feet is heard on the stairs.

In truth it is enjoyable to plate up better food than was had here yesterday for these two mannies. I put a wedge of bread on the side and Comfort rubs his hands in anticipation. No words pass between us as I wipe yesterday's tray and lay out the food.

I add the two china cups of tea, prepared with a plant that Hannah pointed me to in the forest. "Is the master afflicted with stiffness of the joints like you, Comfort?"

Comfort frowns and seems to stoop a bitty more. "He has a lot of pain."

"Well, this might help," I tell him, and off he goes.

I fetch the woven blanket I found last night in a closet, wrap it all around me like a plaid and off I go to look for this 'cook house' that Comfort mentioned yesterday. The track I arrived on the day before continues past our house and on between the trees and tobacco. Trees and tobacco. Trees and tobacco. On and on I go.

Finally I catch sight of wee roofs, all spread out between the trees. So many of them. The track takes a turn downhill and I get a better look at the accommodations before me. Wee huts and big huts. Everywhere. Workers are heading out into the fields, if they can be called fields. It actually feels like just one enormous bit of the world covered in the large leaved plants.

As I get nearer to what seems to really be a village, a plantation village I suppose, I see that there are other crops growing nearby and this puts me in hopes of fresh produce for my mannies. I stop a woman as she walks towards the tobacco and she does look most affa alarmed. I smile at her and explain that I am from the house, pointing back along the way I have come. Her eyes widen some more.

"Is there a 'cook house' or someone I could see about the daily provisions that we get delivered to the house?"

She looks positively terrified now and I know she wants to flee into the field.

"It's all right," I say. "I will find my way."

And off she shoots. I now wonder if I am looking such a terrible sight that people are feart of me. It's a fact that I did not brush my hair this morning; I just got straight up and explored. I try and smooth it down a bit now because I think I have found the right building. There is both smoke and steam coming from its chimney and door, and the air around it fair sings with food.

I knock and a wee quine opens the door more fully. She's holding a long straggly doll and sucking her thumb and she does remind me a bit of Thomas for a moment and I just stand there and stare. She turns and looks back into the room and says, "White lady."

There's immediate noise and movement at this announcement and two women appear in the doorway; they usher the child away and look at me in question.

I smile, again wishing I had brushed my hair. "I'm from the house back there," I tell them, pointing to the way I came. "Is this the right place to ask about the bread and cheese that is delivered there each day?"

It's the older woman that answers, herself brushing down her skirt and apron. "Yes, madam. We do sort that for them, that is, for you."

I have never been called 'madam' before. I'm a quine, a girl, a wee lassie, not some old woman! It takes me back a bit, but I quickly hold out my hand and say, "My name is Beth. I am the new cook at the house and I wonder if there's any way we could get more foods? Meat? Eggs? Milk? Vegetables?"

This causes a bit of a stir between the two women.

"You mean you doesn't get that from town?" asks the older woman.

I shake my head. "No."

"You's been living on bread and cheese?"

And the way she says 'you's' is just the way Eppy would say it at home. In Scotland. And oh, the shame of it, without meaning to, I burst into tears.

Chapter Eighteen

"Oh, Miss Beth, Miss Beth," says the older woman, and the sheer kindness of her actually makes the crying situation worse because it reminds me of how kind Peter was… and of being on the ship with him… and Maggie, who was kind too… and it all explodes out of me like shot from a musket.

I sit on a bench in the wee house. And I cry and cry. Finally, I calm when the wee quine gives me her dolly to hold and I realise I am probably causing much distress to the workers in the cook house.

"I am most affa sorry," I tell them. "I really did just come to ask about the food."

"So you's living in the house with the master and that Comfort," says the older woman, who I've gathered is called Rebecca. She has a motherly feel to her. And that is really why she reminds me of Eppy. Because that's how Eppy felt. To me. "Are they treating you harsh?" Rebecca asks.

"Oh no," I tell her and I explain how I'm feeling sad about Eppy. And Scotland. And Peter. And I tell them all about the kidnapping and the ship.

"My, my," says the younger woman. "That's quite a tale, Miss Beth. I have heard tell of white women being kidnapped before though."

"Oh, there were lots of us, and many many bairns… children that is."

The women shake their heads and glance at each other.

"Well, Miss Beth, we can sort the food. We will give you the same rations we give the Fo'man. He eats a bit grander than the rest of us. And I'm thinkin' Comfort will like that."

A wee chill passes through me at the word 'Fo'man'. It has something of the feel of 'fo'c'sle' about it.

"Comfort seems to like what I've made so far." And I tell them about the onion tart and the fish and the mushrooms.

"You must have been up early, Miss, to catch fishes and find mushrooms," exclaims the younger woman.

I just nod, and it seems to be enough for her.

"That Comfort thinks himself above the rest of us," says Rebecca. "Has you noticed that, Miss Beth?"

"Well, he is the only one who's allowed upstairs," I tell them and they do find this most awfully funny. They don't think I should go and speak to the Fo'man like Comfort suggested. It's the cook house that sorts everybody's food. The wee quiney, who tells me her name is Mary, shows me a barrel of sweet potatoes: everybody gets one with a chunk of bread and a bit of cheese and whatever else is available on the day. Today they are making apple dumplings and this is to be a treat. The apples she points to look rather wrinkled and maggoty. She goes on: "Meat is only for special, but sometimes we gets it in the cook house. We eats better in the cook house. I knead the bread every day."

A thought occurs: "Will we be taking from the workers if we have extra up at the house?" They seem to have so little to begin with. Maybe I actually should see the Fo'man about getting things from town, like they thought we were already doing.

"No, no," says Rebecca. "We'll sort it," and they begin to pack up my basket with what I'm sure is the best of the apples and a sugar loaf and some potatoes and a large piece of ham. I can make broth with it. Like in Scotland. In fact I am sure good Scottish fare will improve the health of the mannies in the house.

"Maybe it will, maybe it won't," says the younger woman when I voice the thought. "There's some things are not so easily mended."

"Shh, Nivvie," says Rebecca.

I ask about porridge, and some dried Indian corn is found, like Mr Lay used. I should soak it overnight, so they tell me. They give me greens and something called okra for my broth. We always did eat rather old fashioned in the castle, but broth with the meat cooked right in it is fortifying. Easy to make, easy to eat. That's what Eppy used to say about it.

And so, I set off back to the house, after Nivvie has checked that the Fo'man is not around. I get the impression he's a man that women should stay away from, and I do appreciate the concern shown for my safety by the lassies of the cook house.

It's quite late to be starting the broth, but the meat is already roasted and the vegetables don't take long. The okra is a strange thing, like nothing I have encountered before. It covers my fingers in some sort of clear slime which, unfortunately, makes me think of slugs and snails. But it thickens the soup up something bonny and makes it more substantial, like barley would have done at home. *Home.* Oh, to be making broth at home. In the castle kitchen. With Peter there too. He's never eaten anything that I made. Does he even know that I can cook? I don't think so. He probably thinks me too grand a lady for that. I do so regret not telling him more about myself, about my life before the boat. And for not asking more about his experiences too. I want to know everything about Peter, my true love, the boy I have to find, and when I do find him, I will make sure to learn it all.

Comfort watches me plate up the broth and put their usual bread and cheese next to it. The bread is soft and good. I make a mental note to tell Wee Mary that next time I visit the cook house, as she was the one who kneaded it. It is not her fault that Comfort left it out in the air to get stale the other day.

"So who did you see down there?" asks Comfort now. "Henderson?"

"I saw Rebecca and Nivvie and a wee quiney in the cook house called Mary. They're going organise the provisions."

"Old Rebecca," he says, and I think I detect the hint of a smile. "How she looking?"

"Good," I say, not quite sure what he means. "Healthy."

"For sure, for sure," he says, nodding. "She always was healthy. So what's this we're having?"

I tell him it's Scottish broth, though in truth the ingredients are a bit different, but he likes the idea and fair scampers away up the stairs to the master with it. Well, he disna really scamper, but for him, he seems to have a bit more of a spring in his step. I must keep making that tea for them, my two auld mannies.

But I also mustn't forget my mission, my aims and my goal; I'm getting lost in the cooking, and enjoying seeing people liking to eat it.

I have to find my way home. I must continue to write letters and get them sent on different ships to make sure they find their way to my father. I must find my dear love Peter. Who knows what situation he now finds himself in? A 'one sweet potato a day' ration situation, like the servants here? So really, I must go into town and enquire around. I'll have to find out how this could be achieved, whether a cart goes there on a regular basis, or if I could borrow a horse and travel on my own. I don't know how these things work around here at all. I bet Rebecca would know. And seeing as how I used all the water in the broth, and have little firewood left, and need to make arrangements about these things, there's no better time to go and ask about town too.

So, wrapping my plaid-like blanket round my shoulders, I set off, back down to the plantation village.

Chapter Nineteen

The sun is shining. The sky is blue. There's a slight smell of smoke as I stroll along the track, cooking smoke, but not the quines' campfire. That scent was different. Distinct. As is the sound I hear as I get nearer to the village.

It is a woman screaming. Screaming and then stifling it. What on earth? Panic rises and I start to run. I run past the tobacco as it sways in the warm breeze, and past the cook house and on towards the terrible sound to which another has added itself. The crack of a whip. I know that noise from when we were herded like animals into the hold of The Planter during the storm. But I have never seen any scene the like of which I look upon now, my feet coming to a sudden standstill as I behold it.

A woman is tied by her wrists to a wooden post that is embedded in the ground. Like a pillory. That is my first thought. It's a place of punishment. A man is whipping her. And whipping her. The man is drenched with the sweat of his exertions while her back is running with blood. Her dress is torn and hanging low, her breasts on display to the small crowd of onlookers. Her belly is also to be seen and it is clear that she is with child.

"Stop this at once!" My words sound out in a bellow worthy of Mrs Sour, so enraged am I. And they are obeyed.

The man stops and, whip raised ready, turns to face me.

"How dare you treat a woman so?" I shout. "There is no crime she can have committed to deserve such treatment!"

"Who the hell are you?" he snarls, still keeping the whip raised, which only serves to rile me up further.

"I am Lady Elizabeth Manteith of the castle of the Shire of Aberdeen in Scotland. And you are going to cut this woman free now."

I take some steps towards him. He lowers his whip. He looks round and another man walks forward. Without words there seems to be some sort of enquiry as to who I am, and the giving of an order, and the woman is untied.

I rush over as she falls to the ground and wrap my plaid around her for decency and comfort and warmth. She turns her face to me. "Miss Beth, you shouldna…"

"Nivvie!" I say, shocked to recognise her in a place where I know so few people. But it means I know where to take her; I know she needs to be in the cook house with Rebecca. I turn us away from the evil mannies and their whips and staring eyes, and we walk, arms about one another to the cook house. I hear people questioning who I am and where I appeared from. I also hear some deliberation that maybe I am a grand visitor to the house, related to the family maybe. Ha! Let them think I am important. Let them be afraid.

"Oh, Nivvie. Oh, Nivvie."

Nivvie's care is taken over by Rebecca and I do soon know what the matter was. She is not meant to be with child. But the child is that of the Fo'man. And it was he who was whipping her. I cannot understand it. I do, however, soon understand that I have been a stupid child myself. A blind and naïve child even.

Nivvie lies on a cot, all curled up like a wee babe, and Rebecca cleans her back.

"Miss Beth, I know you done what seemed right," says Rebecca. "But I think you gone and brought a whole lot more trouble down on Nivvie and maybe some on yourself too."

"But it's the Fo'man who should be in trouble."

"Child. Look around you. Look at the colour of the faces before you."

I still don't understand. There's many dark skinned people here, I know that. It's a big difference from Scotland where our population is very white indeed. Though there are plenty white folk here too.

"He can do what he likes," says Nivvie. "Slaves don't have no rights."

"Slaves?"

"For sure," says Rebecca. "Every black face you see here is a slave."

"But…" and I utter some things that are pure stupidity, exposing the slow workings of my mind. I say that I thought there were no slaves here. I was indentured and I was set free. So the colour of my skin has affected the way I've been treated. I turn this fact over in my mind with everything else I've witnessed and learned on this plantation so far. "But Comfort is free. Isn't he?"

"Comfort is a free man," agrees Rebecca. "He has reason to think himself above the rest of us."

Nivvie lets out a moan, and then goes limp, her hand hanging down from the cot.

"She has passed out," Rebecca tells us, me and Wee Mary who sits on the floor clutching her doll to her chest. "It's for the best; sleep will help her."

I am so angry. But it is a cold and busy anger, an organised anger. "Bar that door when I am gone," I say, wanting to make sure my actions cause no more harm. "I will be back in a bit."

"Now, Miss Beth, don't you go making no more trouble."

"I'm going to talk to Comfort," I say, and it's true, at least it is part of the truth. My other intentions are completely clear by the time I get back to the house. I call for Comfort and wait with extreme impatience while he walks down the stairs. "There's something I'm not sure about, Comfort."

"What's that, Miss Beth?"

"It's through here; maybe you could look at it and explain it to me."

He follows me back into the fine room with the china closet. I dart straight back out and turn the large key in the lock.

"I'm going to speak to the master," I tell him through the door and off I go.

Chapter Twenty

The sound of Comfort's rage is loud as I climb the stairs and then wonder where to go. There's a window at the top of the staircase but the rest of the place seems to be in darkness. The quiet is strange, slow and sluggish. And then I recognise the smell. The black drops. Laudanum. It's horrifying, and sick-making and only associated with bad things, so it does nothing to improve my mood.

However it does show me where to go. I follow the scent into what is obviously a bedchamber and then I see him through the intense gloom of the room, a man laid back in a bed. He's still, unmoving, probably in that half drunken sleep of the poppy.

"So you're the one who says you don't want no more slaves?" I say.

There's a twitch, something, some slight movement in the bed that lets me know he's awake and listening. And I let him have it: about what I've just seen, the atrocity of a woman beaten, possibly a woman raped for all I know, a woman carrying the baby of the Fo'man, a cruel and vicious man who is in the employ of this one in the bed.

The man doesn't reply or move anymore, and I really want to see him, and for him to see me, and for him to understand the true terribleness of the situation, so I walk to the window and try to pull the drapes back. They won't budge. I end up having some sort of fight with them which results in them tearing a bit and me becoming even angrier. The sun is in my eyes, making me have to squint, and I still can't see the man.

I march back and forth in the dark room and shout at him about the Laudanum. How I've smelled it before and I know what it does. It lets a person ignore all that matters around them while they lie there in their little dream land. "You are the master of this place. You are a slave owner who says he wants no more slavery. Will you not go and look? Will you not dismiss the evil man you employ to whip people? Will you not try to help? You must make enough money off of their labours." I pause to catch my breath and then answer for him. "No, you won't. Aye, I ken your type. You'll just lie there, happy on your drops, and let another old man traipse up and down the stairs to bring you food. Meanwhile, outside, beatings and killings and all sorts are going on, or could be going on, and YOU DINNA CARE A WHIT! Arggh!" I pull at my own hair, so enraged am I. "What is the point? And they don't even have enough to eat while the Fo'man has plenty."

With that, off I storm down the stairs, a lot faster than Comfort ever does. Oh aye, Comfort. He's rattling that door something fierce now. The poor old man has shouted himself hoarse. I do start to feel some remorse about that. He is not the slave owner. Or the one with a whip. He's just a servant. Like me. Though he was once a fully owned slave. I go and let him out.

"What was you doing?" he demands, his voice all hissy and worn out. "What was you saying to him?"

"Telling him how one of his slaves was whipped today."

That makes him pause a moment, though I can tell he wants to attempt some sort of rush up the stairs. "Who was that? Who was whipped?"

"Nivvie. She is with child. The Fo'man's child. He had her stripped half naked and tied to a post."

His head goes down and his mouth goes hard, his shoulders more hunched over than ever. He shakes his head as if to remove the image I have put there. "But the master," he says and away he goes.

I walk through to the kitchen, feeling myself begin to calm after the storm. What to do now? Should I go back and see about Nivvie? Or... should I get ready to leave? My father would have sacked any servant who behaved the way I just did. I may be living with the quines, under the stars, by tonight. Or I could find myself being locked up, beaten, and tied to the post. Well I canna stay here to wait for that.

I pour the remaining bit of broth into a lighter pot with a lid and walk out the back door with it. I dinna have many things to gather. I only have this one dress and the one I got to be sold in, and I can leave that behind. I can wash this better dress out in the lake with the quines, as needed. But first, I'm taking this soup to Nivvie. Eppy always said broth was a healing food, and Nivvie is the one in most need of that nourishment.

The forest seems quieter than usual to the one side of me while the tobacco moves in the breeze on the other, but there's not a soul to be seen in among any of it. It's the same story when I reach the village. Of course I have only visited the place twice, but I saw some folks going about on both occasions. Now, there's no one. Just empty spaces between the wee hoosies and buildings, and there's only deathly quiet from the crop.

I knock on the door of the cook house and then add, quietly in keeping with the feel of the place this afternoon, "It's me, Beth."

The door opens a crack and then enough to admit me, and in I go. Nivvie is sitting up on the cot, Wee Mary with her.

"Has there been any other trouble?" I ask.

"Not as yet," says Rebecca, sharing out the broth I brought between four bowls. "But I reckon we'll all need our strength soon. Eat up."

My broth is good. It's not the same as at home but it's nice. Partly because the ham is tasty and that was prepared by Rebecca. So it is that we're exchanging cooking compliments and dipping day old bread in the last of the soup when the door crashes open and the Fo'man drags me out of the cook house by my hair.

Chapter Twenty-one

I fight him all the way. All the way to the whipping post.

Rebecca follows along. "Mr Henderson, sir, Miss Beth didn't rightly know what she was coming into here."

"Well, she's gonna get herself some learnin' then, int she?" he growls, struggling to keep hold of me. "Go back to the cook house, Nigra!"

I try to say to Rebecca to obey and get herself back to safety, but I am shoved up against the post with such violence it takes my breath away. I try to keep fighting; I almost manage to kick Henderson between the legs, as I once did to my cousin Matthew when he was in a particularly foul mood, but the Fo'man has two other men with him now, and they pull my arms around behind me and tie them behind the post. Nivvie was tied the other way, facing it, or maybe she turned with what they did to her. I'm about to find out. Henderson raises his whip high above his head and I flinch, turning to the side and shutting my eyes, bracing for the crack and the impact.

The noise that comes isn't right. It's not that crack sound of the whip, and there's no pain; nothing touches me at all. Just a thunk noise, which for a second makes me think of Comfort's feet on the hollow wooden stairs.

"What the—?" says the Fo'man, and I open my eyes.

It seems that Henderson has just been hit over the head with a stick. A smart gentleman's walking stick. A smart gentleman's walking stick currently being held by a tall, slim, smart gentleman. He has a long blue coat and one of those three cornered hats. And his face is most affa angry.

"You will stop what you are doing here, and you will leave."

That's what the gentleman says. And we all just stare at him, open mouthed.

Henderson, hand rubbing his head, eyes staring at the smart gentleman, is the first to speak: "It is my duty to discipline the workers, sir."

"Beth is not your worker. Nor is it, nor has it ever been, your duty to beat women, or anyone for that matter. I won't have it. Your service here has come to an end."

There's a silence after this. Everyone's thinking their own thoughts, I suppose. I'm thinking: how does this man know my name? Is he a friend of Mr Lay's? If so, how fortuitous a time he did choose to visit. That must be it. Mr Lay did say he would keep an eye on me.

More people are gathering. The crowd is growing every moment; they're coming out of the crop and out of the buildings to watch what's happening at the tying post.

"Untie her at once," says the smart gentleman, and the two who tied me up do as he says. "Are you all right, Miss Beth?" asks the man. "Have you been harmed?"

"I am mostly all right," I say, rubbing my wrists and running my hands back through my manhandled hair, before looking up into the face, the young and handsome face, of the stranger. I feel myself flush, so look away again quickly. The man has very dark brown eyes. And golden hair showing under the hat. And skin that suggests he likes the outdoors. No wig, as some men wear when out and about.

The gentleman surveys the crowd. "Good day to you all," he says, then recognising at least two of the workers because he names them: "Sam," and "Henry."

Sam and Henry step forward, one of them smiling at the gentleman as if pleased to see him.

"You two are in charge now: Sam in the fields, Henry up here."

"You cannot leave a negro in charge of anything," snarls Henderson. "You'll be killed in your beds, the lot of you."

"Henry and Sam, you will accompany Mr Henderson to his house to clear it of his belongings, and then see that he is driven into town. Any wages owed will be forwarded to you."

This last he says to the Fo'man who does not much like it; he turns on his heel real quick and marches away, a grim expression on his face.

"Everybody else," says the fine gentleman. "I am much aggrieved that there has been mistreatment here. Please do take the rest of this day and tomorrow as a holiday, and know that rations will be doubled up from now on. I shall go to the cook house now with Rebecca and Miss Beth to discuss these arrangements."

No one says anything. Sam and Henry are gone with Henderson. Everyone else stays standing around like they don't know what to do, like the time off might be a cruel trick. But we three turn and head to the cook house. We walk quite slow; I realise the gentleman's stick is not just for fashion. He needs it and is leaning on it quite heavily. He is also shaking a wee bitty.

"Miss Beth," says Rebecca to me. "You run on ahead and tell Nivvie we coming."

I lift up my skirt and run, and what a stir my news does cause.

"Who is a-coming?" Nivvie asks when I tell her the news.

"A fine gentleman. He has sacked Mr Henderson and put Sam and Henry in charge of the fields and up here."

"And this gentleman is coming here, now?"

"Aye," I assure her. "He walks with a stick, so they'll be a wee minty."

We move quickly round the cook house, myself more quickly than poor Nivvie in her recently beaten state, cleaning up and getting a chair ready for the gentleman, and putting on water for tea, and looking out some good cake. Wee Mary helps too, slicing the cake up neatly.

I keep causing Nivvie to stop in astonishment as I tell her more of what took place. "A holiday?" she says. "And what are we to do in the winter if we double the rations now?"

There is no time to deliberate on this, for Rebecca and the gentleman are here. He is shown to the chair, which I can see he is very glad to ease down onto. He looks to be in a bit of a sweat.

Nivvie has the tea on. The cake is laid out ready.

"Now, Master Michael," says Rebecca. "This a right to-do you've started today."

Master Michael? I look at the man and words blurt straight out of my mouth. "But the master is an auld mannie, nae a young and handsome one!" Oh, to be able to snatch your speech back. Rebecca and Nivvie find it most amusing. And Master Michael? He just smiles a small smile, and as my face turns as bright a colour as my hair, he turns the conversation to food.

Chapter Twenty-two

We are to order in more rice and dried beans to make up a better bulk of food for everyone, including us up at the house. More land is to be given over to the growing of food for eating here. Rebecca suggests having more pigs. I suggest buying in oats.

"We ate them all the time back in Scotland; they are cheap and they do not take much cooking," I say, glad to be talking sensibly and perhaps being of some use. "They do make a filling breakfast. And a good stuffing with onions for meat. And even bannocks, fresh wee breads done over the fire."

Michael does not know if oats are easily available but there will be a trip to town soon to order provisions, so people are not to worry about using up the rations.

"I did not know you were going hungry," says Michael. "Not until Beth here told me this afternoon."

I flush again at the memory of that, but do not apologise. For what I said was true. And good things are now happening because of it.

"In truth I have not been going very hungry here in the cook house," says Rebecca, laughing and patting her ample middle. "But it'll be good to know every man and woman and child is going to bed with a full belly." She pauses, looking at Michael. "It must be ten years since I've seen you, sir," she says. "And what a fine young man you've grown into. That Comfort must have been doing something right."

"He's a good man," says Michael.

Rebecca grunts. "Just twelve you were when you came here with him? Is that right?"

"It is," says Michael.

Rebecca shakes her head. "Just a boy, so recent lost his daddy."

"It may be time for me to be heading back," says Michael, standing slowly and leaning on the stick again.

"Oh, but we'll fetch you a horse and waggon," says Rebecca. "Mary, run down to the stable and tell the man there the master is needing a cart to get home. And Miss Beth too." She calls this last bit out the door after the wee lass who is already running off from the house at quite a speed.

"Now," says Rebecca, turning to me. "There's been a deal of good work done today. The master'll be needing a hearty supper. I'll give you some salt pork to make a pie for him."

"Oh, no need for such bother," says Michael. "Just some bread will do."

Rebecca and I both shake our heads at this and I agree with her about the pie. I recall how good pork pie was with a bit of pickle, maybe an apple, some cheese… "Or I could make a gravy with some of the fat, and serve it with potatoes and the last of the greens you gave me…" I muse, feeling quite hungry myself.

By the time we leave in the cart, both Michael and myself having been lifted up onto it by the two men who brought it, I have promised to save a slice for Nivvie so she can see how a Scottish pie tastes. In my mind I decide to make three small pies, one for each of my cook house friends. Or maybe five little pies, one each for the quines too. And if they're not about, it would be something extra for Michael and Comfort in the morning, or with their broth.

We trundle along in silence for a wee minty. We meet a group of men coming back along the road, from the fields I assume. I don't know if they ken they've got a day off now. A day off from their… slaving. Rebecca told me that every black face here is a slave. And this group of men are black. And I am sitting right beside their owner, who is now to see that they have more to eat, and that the cruel fore-manny is gone… but Michael still owns them. He owns people. And no amount of being young and handsome can take that away from him.

So I stay silent. I will look after him and Comfort as best as I can. Until I go home. To Eppy and Jock and my father. I have to go home to them. I have to find Peter. I have to write many many letters and make enquiries wherever I can think to. These are the things that matter. These are the people that must matter most to me.

"I am not a slave owner," says Michael, as if to argue with my thoughts. He sounds tired as he turns towards me, where we sit, legs dangling from the cart. "My mother owns everything you see here. I was able to free Comfort because he was given to me as my own. As were your indentures. But she controls everything else, including me."

"Wait a minute," I say, because... hang on just a minty. "Mrs Sour is your mother?"

"Oh yes," he says, and it's a loaded 'yes'.

"And she left you here alone at the house when you were twelve?"

"It made sense," he tells me. "She didn't want to see me, and I didn't want to see her. I do the accounts for the place but I am here to run it too and it shall be better run from now on."

I nod. I believe him.

"And when she dies?" he says. "Well... things will change further."

I do regret the plan to make quite so many pies when I am halfway through the task. But once they're done? Well, they're just lovely. Bonny and browned on top; I am growing quite fond of the wee bread oven. Such tasty pies, they don't need gravy. So I serve them up with cheese and bread and the tea to help my mannies, one old, and one not so old, as it turns out.

Comfort was in a terrible state when we arrived back at the house. I think he'd even been crying, so worried was he.

"Everything is all right," Michael assured him, putting his hands on the old man's shoulders. "But I am right tired now and would appreciate some help getting up the stairs."

By the end of the day I am right tired too. But there's one thing I'm realising as I get all sleepy and warm in my wee box bed. It's never boring here. No sheer. No utter. No boring at all. And that is my last thought before I fall asleep.

Chapter Twenty-three

"Miss Beth! Miss Beth!" It's Comfort and he's in a worse state than earlier, and he's come right into my bedchamber, the sheer and utter cheek of it!

I quickly realise he has good reason. Something terrible is happening.

"It's the master! It's the master!" he says, turning and taking off towards to stairs. I wrap a blanket around myself, being only in my under garments, and follow him. "He wouldn't take his drops last night," Comfort tells me. "Says he's done with that. But now I think he's dying."

He may be. He's convulsing. Right there on the bed. Head bent right back. Back arched. In the candlelight. Just like my wee brother. Thomas. Right before he died. For a moment I am frozen between the two times of then and now. But all at once I know exactly what to do. "We have to get Laudanum into him," I shout at Comfort. "You canna come off it all at once. It has to be done gradual like. Come on, come on!"

We get the bottle of dark dreams. Comfort holds Michael's head and I force, probably too much, of the liquid into his mouth and then try to hold his jaw closed. At first it seems it has not worked, but after a while he quiets and his body relaxes and his breathing becomes easy again. I am so relieved. And sorry. And sad. I burst right into tears there on the bed.

"You done good, Miss Beth," says Comfort. "He be all right now."

"He nearly died. And it was because I shouted at him about the drops. Without telling him anything else he needed to know." So I tell

Comfort what I should have told Michael before. How you reduce it a wee bitty for a few days and then a wee bitty more a few days later. You have to go real slow. But, no matter what you do, it disna always work. My father tried to get my mother to stop. Several times. And then he gave up.

"Master Michael is young," says Comfort. "It should go better for him."

"I know," I say. "I said he was young and handsome, in front of him today, such a shock it was to learn that this was him, the master, who I'd thought was old. But what an embarrassment." I shake my head at the memory.

"Having a young lady say you're handsome doesn't hurt anybody," Comfort assures me.

"He didn't look like a person on Laudanum when he appeared down at the plantation," I say, because he really didn't. Even now he doesn't. My mother was so pale, her skin like crumpled paper. Michael's complexion is darker, in striking contrast to his light curled hair, like someone who has been out and about under the sun plenty, not a man who's been shut in his room for years.

"You've had some effect on him, Miss Beth. He's not been the same since you barged in here. I'm ashamed to say it was me started him on them drops. He was so hurted himself, and his father had just died. He was waking every night screaming. They made him feel better. They let him sleep. But they don't keep working the same. He's needed more and more as time's gone on."

I nod, familiar with that as well. Another memory stirs as I brush Michael's hair back from his forehead and feel his face to see how hot he is. He's cool. "Chocolate might help him. It lifts the spirits." And another memory pops up. "Mr Lay said there is a shop in Philadelphia where I can buy it."

"Well, when the master is better, we can ask him if you can go."

Oh, I'm going. It does not matter what any manny tells me, master or no. I need to get chocolate for Michael, and to ask around about Peter, and to send another letter to my father. As it turns out it is much easier than expected to arrange the trip.

The next morning, Michael appears as I am preparing the yellow corn porridge. He is looking much better than last I saw him, obviously. He is drawn about the face, but more relaxed than the day before, in plainer shirt and trews. I knew it was not Comfort's feet I heard coming down the stairs. Even with the stick, the young man is quicker than the old man. The old man who I suspect must be still asleep, else he would be down here too.

"Comfort mentioned I gave you some trouble in the night?" asks Michael.

And I give him the talk about the Laudanum and how you have to come off it slow, real slow.

He frowns. "I would prefer to be done with it at once."

"Well, ye canna." And because that seems a bit bossy and rude of a way for me to be talking to my master, I phrase the next piece of advice as a question: "Will you sit at the table to eat breakfast, sir?"

"Yes, yes," he says, pulling out a chair and sitting. "We should leave Comfort to get his rest; he's gone back to sleep now. But please, call me Michael. There cannot be much difference in the ages between you and me?"

"I am… seventeen years old." I almost said sixteen, that being the age I am used to telling people. But I know my birthday has passed, perhaps on the boat, maybe on the island, maybe even while I was walking along the street holding Peter's hand. And there can be no doubt. I am now seventeen.

His mouth opens, shocked. "You're little more than a child!"

"I can assure you, I am not a child," I say, somewhat infuriated.

"But, you are very young. I thought you much older."

For a moment I am pacified and pleased to have been thought of as older than I am, possibly for the first time in my life. But then I am slightly saddened also, as this probably means the kidnapping, the journey, and all that has happened, has aged me. Michael, of course, does not know any of my story. Well, he soon does, which makes him all the more shocked. He is in full agreement that we must find out about Peter when I tell of the heroic behaviour that saved both my virtue and my life. I do not tell all the details of that incident, fully formed though they are in my mind. My hands pushing a man. My hands killing a man. There are more important things to be done now than dwelling on what happened on the boat.

The plan for the trip into town springs naturally from all this and Michael wants it to happen soon, real soon, he says. He is going to pay for notices to be printed and put up around town to aid in the quest to find my true love, though I did not tell him the true love part. And I am to have new dresses. And fine herbs from the good shops hereabouts to make my cooking more Scottish, more how I like it. We are to sup at a tavern and have a wonderful time. It is, in fact, going to be a grand day out!

We eat our porridge. I give Michael black tea, thinking anything uplifting and stimulating like that might help him. He is bright enough but I can see that he tires easily, though he does insist in helping me with the plates and the pies for the quines in the cook house. My own quines are nowhere near today again. I determined that by the outside air when I first got up. Maybe they have moved on to another area. I ken that they don't like to stay in one place for too long.

Comfort is not impressed with the plans for the day out. He says it is too soon. For Michael. And he may be right. But Michael insists that he will go and sit in a tavern after the print shop. I can take someone to help me from the village, maybe Nivvie if she wants to go, if she is recovered enough, and I can do the dress shopping by myself.

"You don't know what you's asking him to do," says Comfort once Michael has gone upstairs. "Getting him up and about is one thing, putting him in a waggon is another."

"He was in a cart yesterday to come back from the village."

"Not driving it," says Comfort. "Not sitting up front like he will be on this trip." And then he will say no more.

Chapter Twenty-four

It is three days until we go on our trip, Michael, Nivvie and me. Comfort is still fretting about the fact that Michael has been mainly in his room for ten years, can hardly sleep on the reduced Laudanum, and how everything is changing too fast for him. The 'him' he means is Michael, but I wonder if it's really Comfort who's finding the altered circumstances disturbing. Michael seems quite happy, and Comfort should not be allowed to cling on to how things have been here just for his own peace of mind.

"If we dinna de it noo," I say, hearing my language get more Scottish in my agitation and then toning it down a bit to make sure I'm understood, "it may be that Michael retreats back into his room and back onto those drops. He wants to go now, and we're going."

"Well, there's things you should know first."

I wait, expectantly, to be told of the 'things'. I raise my eyebrows and consider tapping my foot, so long is it taking the old man to tell me.

"But the master wouldn't want you to know."

"All right then." And that's it. I am not told.

Nivvie arrives, all excited about the trip, as I am myself.

"You're quite sure you're recovered enough to go?" I ask.

"Oh yes, I'm healing up just fine," she assures me. "And this is a mighty fine house you have here, Miss Beth." I can tell by the way she glances curiously around that she would like to see more, so I show her round the downstairs. She is impressed with my box bed and the finer room with the fancy furniture and all the lovely plates and cups. And then Michael appears and I didn't even hear him come down. He's just there when I close up the china cabinet right after Nivvie and I had just been having some fun examining all the contents. I feel a bit embarrassed, not knowing how long he's been there or if he listened to us discussing the pretty floral design of the plates and saying how some of them looked like weeds that grow in the woods. But by his smile, and the friendly way he greets Nivvie, I can tell that he is really looking forward to this day and not thinking I was being silly or behaving like the house was mine or anything. The excitement in his face makes him look younger, as if he really were the same age as me.

He is dressed even more smartly than when he turned up at the village, wearing a different coat and hat but the same stick. He gets up into the front of the cart quite easily by himself, and I join him there, trying to ignore the fact that Comfort is standing beside the horse, wringing his hands and generally behaving as if doom is about to fall down on all our heads.

"I can do it, Comfort," says Michael.

The old man immediately tries to behave like he believes this too. "I know it, Master Michael. I know it."

Nivvie insists on riding in the back of the cart, though there is plenty room up front with us. I worry that she might not be comfortable back there, though she insists that she is. Unconvinced, I try to persuade her to join us at the front, to no avail.

"Are we ready to go yet, ladies?" asks Michael, and I worry that he's feeling a bit impatient with us, or at least with me, for delaying the journey.

Turning to him, I'm relieved to see a small smile, like a teasing smile, on his face.

"Aye, we're ready," I say.

His smile broadens as he flicks the reins and, off we go.

Comfort shouts advice after us like, "Be home before dark!" and "Watch out for the big dips in the road!"

"We will!" Michael shouts back, smiling again. This really is a very happy day.

And Michael really is a very handsome man. He has one of those jaws that is clearly defined and square looking. High bones in his cheeks too. He looks round at me and I look away, embarrassed to be caught staring, but then we get to talking and everything feels good again. First we talk about the things we are seeing: the different trees and plants and birds. He wants to know how the countryside is in Scotland and I tell him how there, by the castle anyway, we are mainly surrounded by ancient oak woods.

Michael is most interested to hear about the castle and soon he knows all about the various rooms of the place, and the furniture, and the Mermaid and the Bear, and then my wee brother, and how he died all of a sudden like. And how everything changed then. My mother took to her room. My father took up his cause. I am probably too loose tongued about that — Jacobites should stay hidden and secret — but here with Michael and Nivvie I feel safe. I even tell them about the carved wooden plums on the fireplace of the great hall.

"The plums down in the orchard are nearly ripe," says Nivvie, who has stayed very quiet up till now. "You could make a sweet pie, Miss Beth."

"We all love Miss Beth's pies," says Michael. "They're the best I've ever tasted. Comfort says they remind him of his mother's cooking, and that's high praise indeed."

"He's never said that to me," I say, though it has been clear that Comfort likes my food.

"Ah, well," says Michael. "He is somewhat afraid of you."

"No!" I'm amazed. "Why?"

There's a short silence, and then Nivvie says, real quick like, "Miss Beth, you are a fiery young woman. Your temperament matches your hair."

They both laugh. The sheer and utter cheek of them! But then I laugh too, for it is most affa funny. "Aye, well, my hair is very badly behaved." I was up before light brushing it today, but I don't tell them that. "It comes from having a mermaid for a great, great, great — I canna mind how many greats — grandmother."

"That must be it," says Nivvie and we all melt into fits of laughter again.

I take a peek at Michael, just to make sure he is not tiring, driving the horse as he is. But he is fine. Mighty fine.

Michael knows just where to go when we reach Philadelphia. He guides us through the red brick buildings, and past the many pretty gardens although I am glad that he does not suggest calling on his mother. That would spoil this sweet day.

I tie up the horse, wishing I had brought an apple or carrot for it; it is a bonny beast, if a bit old and in need of a good brushing. I take my time stroking the horse's nose, only turning when I'm sure Michael will have climbed down from the cart. He smiles at me from his place on the roadside, feet on solid ground, stick by his side, and I know I was right. He wouldn't have welcomed any witnesses to his descent. At least not familiar ones.

Nivvie has also taken her time getting out of the cart, and I wonder if perhaps her wounds are not as well healed as she would have liked me to believe. I step between them, my two injured friends, Nivvie on one side, Michael on the other, and together we cross the street and enter Mr Franklin's printing shop.

Chapter Twenty-five

It is noisy inside the shop. We can hear printing machines running in the back, but there seems to be nobody to see in the front room of the place. Michael goes to search for somebody in the back while Nivvie and I inspect the goods on display. We quickly find the chocolate and into my basket it goes. Five blocks of it. There are indeed bibles and pencils and books, like Mr Lay said there would be. I find a small cooking manual and am perusing it when Michael returns with another man.

Michael introduces Ben Franklin, an old friend of his father's.

"And your friend too, Michael," says the man, then inspecting me over the top of his small spectacles before returning his gaze to Michael. "I am most delighted to see you again, my boy," he continues. "I had no idea at all that you had married."

There's a short pause before Michael and I both correct the mistake.

"I am Mr Sauer's cook," I say, feeling decidedly flustered by what has been said. Not knowing quite what to do with myself, I hold up the cooking manual and hope it hides my warm cheeks. I mean, what an audacious thing to say!

"Ah, no, no," says Michael, also looking somewhat mortified, and glancing at me in a panicked sort of way. "Beth has been helping me, plying me with her pies and potions."

Ben Franklin looks at me directly through his spectacles this time, with what I take to be a twinkle of amusement. "I am sorry," he says, smiling. "The way you spoke of her just now, Michael, I thought… but no matter! I believe there are some letters to be sent to England?"

I think we're all relieved to be moving on to another subject, and I take out the four letters I have written. There are two to be sent to England, two to Scotland, and it is only then, talking to Mr Franklin, that I find myself facing a great truth. I will be in America for a long time. An affa, affa, long time. It took months for me to get here. It will take months for these letters to travel back. Winter is approaching, weather is worsening; that will slow things further. I have written four letters because I do not know where my father will be. One goes to the castle again, like the first one sent by Mr Lay, and one goes to London. Another goes to our property in the North of England and the last one is addressed to our far flung island home in the West. That one will take the longest time to reach its destination. Letters even sometimes get dropped in the sea on their way there.

Then, once the news has finally reached my father, something will have to be arranged. I don't know what. Will I receive a letter back? Will someone come for me? Whichever, whatever, they will take more months to get here. And ships sometimes sink. And letters sometimes just get lost, even if they don't fall in the sea.

"You'll be all right here with us until then," says Nivvie, smiling encouragingly when I express these facts there in the shop.

"I believe there are some notices to be printed also?" says Mr Franklin, and I focus my mind to talk about Peter. I'm not sure I do a very good job. In trying to avoid speaking of him as my true love, I've made him sound like a heroic figure who saved me, and who now needs saving in return, which doesn't sound quite right. No-one seems to notice though and Mr Franklin asks if he could print my story in his newspaper. I agree at once, inconsistencies put aside, for it means more people will read about what happened to us and maybe someone will know of Peter and where he went. For, as I've been telling my story, some dark and confused thoughts have started to form at the back of my mind about my true love. I have no idea how long it will take for me to arrange passage home. I've established that here today. What if I have not found Peter by the time word comes? How could I possibly leave without my dear friend? Yet, how could I refuse to go home?

The most terrible possibility: maybe Peter will never be found. Maybe… my thoughts falter and then I let them go where they're going. Maybe he's already dead at the hands of someone like the Fo'man. I know I have been lucky. I am alive. I have enough food. And a bed to sleep in. I am not being worked to death in a field. Or whipped by a bad man. I know I was a spoilt wee lassie before. I know I am forever changed. But my heart remembers Scotland in a very direct and painful way as I talk it all out here in the printer's shop with the printed papers drying high above us, the smell of the ink and the sound of the printing press in the other room. I talk about my father, and even my mother. Thomas; my wee brother. Prince Charles, the one that really matters to me; my wee dog, not the man who would be rightful king after his father.

Once we leave the shop, after the telling of the sad, sad, tale, I can hardly see the things we are passing in the street. Shops and other buildings are red and grey blurs. People are all I can focus upon. I find myself desperately searching faces to see if they are Peter, even those of wifies and wee bairns. If only he would just show up now, and be safe, and ready to return to Scotland with me.

I take Michael's arm when it is offered, and he comes with us into the dressmaker's shop, though I was meant to do this bit without him. It's like I can see the pretty fabrics and linens, but I can't feel the joy of them. Not properly. I wonder what happened to Prince Charles after I lost him on the quay. Something as bad as happened to me? Something worse?

"This would suit you with your hair," says Nivvie, and I nod. It is a dress already made up, with wee flowers printed on the weave. It will only need a small alteration and I can stay and have it done today. I do not argue. So Michael and Nivvie leave me with the dressmaker and her assistant while they go to see about food things. Rice and beans and seeds and herbs.

I stay here.

I lift my arms for the waist to be pinned. I lower my arms for the shoulders to be changed. I step up on a stool, but the gown is the right length for me, which is a surprise. Usually there's tutting about how tall I am and how more fabric will be needed. But not here. America is a taller place than Scotland, so it seems.

After a while, all I can see is those little blue and green flowers and leaves that make up the print. There is a hat to match. And I do look a proper lady as I stare at myself in the mirror. It is like looking through glass at another person. I never looked like this in Scotland. I've certainly never looked like this here. There are two more dresses coming; they will be delivered. They are to be more like the one I already had on, my servant's attire. For cooking. And cleaning. In my wee house. Michael's wee house.

They are back, Michael and Nivvie, and they are most admiring of my dress. And my hat. And me. It is embarrassing and strange. Nivvie has a new cloak. It is very fine and will fit her no matter how fat she gets. So she tells me. They bought one for me too. They have sorted out the food, which will be delivered to the house and plantation village soon, and now we are to go to the tavern.

The tavern is loud too and, like so many places in this city seem to be, so full of people. I do the face search again, looking for Peter. I mean he could be anywhere. It is hard to stop this activity to eat my food, but when I do, it is so good. We eat chicken and bread, and we drink stronger ale than we have at home, and I begin to feel myself come back to some sort of sense again.

"It was a shock to speak of Scotland like that," I tell my companions. "It is so far away and I had not put all those thoughts together in one go before."

"We'll get you home, Beth," Michael assures me, nodding, his handsome face most serious.

"And we'll look after you till you get there," adds Nivvie.

I have only been here days. I cannot believe it. It feels like forever already. And the time I have left in America will not be measured in days. Or weeks. Months, yes, months. For sure.

Chapter Twenty-six

We sing on the way home. We eat the sweets that we bought at the market we visited after the tavern. Maybe it is the stronger ale that has done this to us, but we are a rowdy wee group, merry even. Once we are out of the city, Nivvie joins us up front, and we arrange ourselves with Michael in the middle, a quine on each side. We none of us know the same songs though, which makes for even more merriment as we try to sing along with words we do not know.

As is the way with all gaiety, it eventually comes to an end. And in this case, it comes to a very sudden and jarring end. I have been checking Michael for signs of tiredness or unwellness, but detect nothing until we approach the house. As we pull up beside another cart that is stopped there he visibly pales. And Nivvie goes quiet. A big black and brown dog jumps down from the porch and runs round and round us, barking something fierce.

Well, this is one problem I can fix. I know I can, and I climb down onto the ground, one of the treats left over from the market in my hand. I am right. The creature likes me; dogs always do. It takes the sweet biscuit from my fingers real gently for such a big and unruly animal.

"Miss Beth, no," says Nivvie in a tone that is both hushed and urgent. "That's the Fo'man's dog, and it's vicious."

"Well, he's my friend now," I say, turning to face them as I play with the dog's ears while he bangs his tail on the ground. I've missed dogs' tails banging on the ground.

Seeing my friends' horrified faces though, helps Nivvie's words sink in. Whose dog did she say this was? I look again at the other waggon that's sitting here, and the horse that's attached to it, and realise that they are really familiar. The woman that's coming out of our house is unpleasantly familiar too. The cheek of her being in there when we were out! Michael's mother is followed by the Fo'man. Henderson. And Sarah too.

Mrs Sour shrieks in rage from where she stands on the porch. "So it's true! My own son has been out to Philadelphia and he didn't even bother to visit his old mother. You should be ashamed. All of you."

The words are out before I can consider them: "Seeing as you're here, how would you know where he's been?"

The old woman turns the colour of a bramble, or blackberry, under her white hair. "Are you going to let your servant speak to me like this, Michael? And what's she doing all dolled up like that? Like she's a lady?"

Michael's two feet hit the dirt beside me and my new doggie friend. I see the small flinch, hidden quickly away like a secret or a smile as is the case sometimes in these parts, and know it has hurt him to jump down like that to face his parent.

"Beth is my friend," he says. "And she actually is a fine lady, mother, from a far finer family than ours. You are the one who should be ashamed. Beth's story is going to be printed in The Gazette."

She says nothing for a moment, appearing to be quite taken aback by this information. Henderson coughs and Mrs Sour speaks again. "You told Mr Henderson to go? What madness is this? He is to be reinstated at once."

"Do I still run this plantation?" demands Michael.

Mother and son stare at each other, neither moving any closer, just standing, glaring, but I sense some sort of communication is taking place nonetheless. A breeze rustles through the trees, lifting my new hat slightly, blowing my hair back, and then the dog barks.

"Well then," says Michael as if his question has been answered. "Run it I shall."

"If profits go down…" says Mrs Sour, "I will replace you."

Michael's answer is swift. "Then my story will go in The Gazette too."

A shudder goes through Mrs Sour like she's about to have some sort of fit, but she doesn't. She strides down off our porch and walks over to her own cart. Mr Henderson follows her, pausing to spit on the ground while looking at us, and then calling his dog which appears to be called, just 'Dog'.

"Dog!" he repeats, looking as sour as Mrs Sour and sounding as vicious as the dog was said to be.

The dog makes a whining noise and stays by me. I keep my hand on the animal's soft head, rubbing his fur, reminding him that I am kind and that maybe he should be mine now.

"Come away from the little whore, you stupid beast," says Henderson, taking a few steps towards us. I feel the dog's hackles rise as the foul man speaks. I think its allegiance has shifted, just as people's are prone to do, especially in war-like situations, or when there is a question of who should be running or ruling a place. I ken this well from all that's going on in Scotland, and I think the dog is mine now.

"Don't speak about Beth like that," says Michael to Henderson.

"What's a cripple like you going to do about it?" asks the Fo'man who then steps in our direction again, his stance unquestionably aggressive.

The dog growls.

"Dog!" says Henderson, like an idiot who doesn't know how to name a dog, and he lunges forward to grab the animal.

The nameless creature darts at Henderson, barking and snarling, and looking as if he might pounce. Henderson uses language I am familiar with, language used by men who kidnap wee bairns and sell them off for profit. And he kicks out at the dog who then takes Henderson's trouser leg in its jaws and pulls, tearing the fabric.

"Fine!" yells the man, quickly retreating and jumping up on the cart with Mrs Sour, and Sarah, who is in the driving position as usual. "Stay with your own kind, you filthy mongrel."

I wave to their cart as it trundles away. "Goodbye!" I shout after it, and them. "We have chocolate and you don't!" I turn to Michael and Nivvie, slightly embarrassed by my words. "It was a bit childish of me to say that, wasn't it?" I ask them.

Nivvie is only now emerging from the back of the cart where I think she must have hidden when she saw Henderson. Seeing her belly protruding from under her new cloak, I am right glad he did not catch sight of her.

"It's true though," I add, reaching up for the basket containing the chocolate and holding up a block of it. "Our lives are about to change for the better, and right now!"

Chapter Twenty-seven

I shave slivers of chocolate from the block and stir them into hot water over the fire. I add sugar and mix until it is all well blended. Then I pour it all into the pot with the warm milk and whisk and whisk until it's frothy and perfect. Nivvie has laid out the finest china cups from the cabinet, the ones with wee flowers on, and the two mannies wait in anticipation.

I know Michael is very tired. I know Comfort is also, having had rather a stress filled day, some of it with Mrs Sour and Henderson, who had him wait on them as if they were royalty, by the sounds of things, and the state of the kitchen. But they shall have chocolate before they go to bed, Michael and Comfort that is, not Sour and Henderson. As if!

We all agree that the chocolate is very good. I am the only one who has had it before and I think it would be a good breakfast drink for us. It raises the spirits and enlivens the body. We eat a simple supper of bread and cheese and apples this night, but we really do feel like kings and queens in our house, with our chocolate, and our fancy cups, and our laughter, and even our tiredness, because it's come from a good day of doings.

Doings that might take me one step closer to going home. Doings that might find Peter. Sarah told Comfort that herself and Mrs Sour are still making enquiries of folks they see in town, though nothing has come of this as yet.

My new dog follows me everywhere I go, maybe because I give him wee bits of every food we're having as I get it ready. I don't give him chocolate though. I don't think that would be good. It does not make a person drunk, but it does something; it has some effect on the mood and I remember cousin Matthew giving wine to my wee Prince Charles once. The poor dog couldn't walk straight after it and I did not share in my cousin's mirth at the fact. So, no chocolate for my new dog. My dog in America. My dog that needs a name.

The name comes before I even open my mouth to ask the advice of my friends. It comes straight into my head as I look at the dog who is big and furry and gentle with me and mine, but can be a fearsome beast when needed. A great bear of a beast. And so he is 'Bear'. He answers to it at once, when I call him, with a bit of leftover pie in my hand right enough, but I ken he knows it is his new name, here in his new home, with his new mistress.

Bear's ribs are far too prominent, but that changes with everything else as the season progresses. One morning I catch a hint of that particular scent of wood smoke at the back door. Bear sniffs the air too. "You know what this means, don't you?" I say to him. He wags his tail excitedly, understanding that it means something good, and we set off through the trees together, taking some chocolate and fresh bread with us for the quines.

It is, indeed, so good to see my two friends again. Bear and I join them at their camp fire and we all share food together. The quines rarely have bread so it is as much a treat to them as their mushrooms are to us.

They are pleased to hear of our visit to Philadelphia and that the bad Fo'man is gone, not that they knew about him before anyway. I sip my chocolate, noticing Eliza's growing belly as we sit and talk round the fire. She is not as far on as Nivvie, but there can be no doubt that she is in the same state. As she says nothing of it, neither do I. They send me home with some spare mushrooms which go nicely with eggs for the mannies' breakfast.

Once a week Michael and I, with Bear, intend to visit the village, or 'Quarters' as Comfort calls the place, and see every person there. 'Village' is the better word, a friendlier word, so I tell Comfort, but he still does not want to go with us. The harvesting of the tobacco is progressing well, regardless of the fact that there is no proper, or frightening, overseer now. The crop is being hung to dry.

Michael stands at the front of the large gathering room, on this, our first visit, and invites people to raise any concerns they may have. At first no one speaks. People look at each other. I notice how the room is divided. The white folks are all at the front together, and I don't much like it.

But it's not a white person that stands to speak. It's Rebecca. She raises the question of church. As things are at the moment, as they have been, only the indentured servants get to go. Each Sunday they have use of the horses and carts to go to church in Philadelphia, and they don't have to work the rest of the day like everyone else. She tells us this fact and then sits back down, leaving us to do what we will with it, not specifically asking for anything.

Michael declares that a free day and church on Sunday is now to be for everyone, but that it is possible we may not have enough transport. People are happy to walk; they say so. They will start early in the morning and picnic on the way. Michael says that women and children are to be given first chance to travel in the carts and everyone seems happy with that.

"Things are not all as they should be," says Michael. "But together we can make it better. Now, I think Beth has some sustenance for us all?"

I do. I've been up since dawn preparing it and uncover it now from under the cloths on the table. There are jugs of chocolate and plates of sliced up blueberry cakes for everyone. I hope there's enough. There's a fair crowd, and they're all keen to see what there is. Rebecca has provided lots of wooden cups for the chocolate, and though I see some people sharing, I think everyone gets some. Bear gets quite a few mouthfuls of cake, especially from the children of the village.

I think about what is happening: people working less hours, people eating more food, all good things. But: "The profit of the farm, the plantation; it's going to go down, isn't it?" I say to Michael as we travel back to the house after the meeting.

"Yes."

"So your mother...?"

"Oh, she won't replace me," he assures me. "I know that for sure. And who knows? People may get more work done when they have more to eat and better treatment. But tell me, Beth, what about church for yourself?"

"I will go along with everyone else," I say, quite looking forward to the outing, and knowing it will provide another chance to look for Peter, to ask about Peter, aye, and to pray for Peter and all things working out in the right time for our safe passage home.

"But with your family being in favour of the Stuart King, does that not mean you are of the old religion?"

"Not all Jacobites are Catholic," I say, keen to correct this misunderstanding. "But aye, we were. Are. We went to the village church like everyone else, but when father was home there was a Mass said in secret too, in an underground chapel."

"There's a Catholic Church in Philadelphia."

"Is that legal?"

"In Penn's city of brotherly love? Yes, it's legal, and I'll happily go there with you myself."

Chapter Twenty-eight

I open my mouth to accept the blood and body of Christ. It is so long since I have done this that a small shudder goes through me, like I've stepped into a memory, and am now somewhere else, somewhere secret and deep underground, far away, on the other side of the world, with my family.

I sit back down with Michael, who does not go forward; of course, he cannot, never having taken communion. But he shakes hands with everyone at the end, and assists me in my enquiries about Peter, and when we walk away from the church, back out into the street, he remarks that he felt the difference in the atmosphere of the place during the event of the Eucharist, when the bread and wine changed. He also noticed the reverent hush that fell over the people, and felt the holiness. His family were Quakers, so they never went to a church as such. They had meetings in houses. And after his father died, his mother converted to the Anglican faith. But Michael had moved to the plantation house by then, with Comfort.

It seems a strange thing to me that a family member would die, and the family then separate. But it happened to us too, to the Manteiths in the castle, so I understand well how such situations arise. Terrible pain spawns many terrible things.

We are soon met with the others and back in the cart, or waggon as Rebecca says we should call it, with the cook house lassies. No one else rides with us, despite there being plenty of room. There's a lot of people thinking they're above and below others in the plantation. White above black. Cook house above field workers and most everyone else. It vexes me a bit to hear of it. Why canna we all just get on? I ask this aloud and

Rebecca laughs. "But you stay in the house with Comfort, the man who thinks he is above us all."

"I don't think he thinks that," I say, because I really don't. I had the feeling this morning that Comfort would have quite liked to come with us, but he's holding back, not out of 'aboveness' but because of some sort of fear or shyness. I wonder if maybe he just hasn't been out of the house for so long, that the thought of being anywhere else is frightening?

But once we are home, Comfort asks us all about our day, and then proceeds to tell us how he took Bear for a walk down to the village; he stresses my word for the place, and remarks on how strange it was, all empty of folk.

"Maybe you should visit when it's not empty?" I suggest, surprised to learn that he could even walk that far, and hoping it could perhaps be the start of his venturing out more. But talk turns to supper and what's to be made; a roast chicken is the plan, and no more is said of Comfort visiting anywhere.

The week now has a pattern to it, which is good as it means I now know what day it is. I sound like a mad lassie to say that, I know, but since the ship I have truly felt one day to be the same as the next, just different in what was occurring… and so much has occurred. Now we have a meeting day, and a church day, and five normal days.

Michael's withdrawal from Laudanum is difficult at night still, though there have been no more fits; I know he does not sleep as he should and his leg gives him much pain. Or this is what Comfort says about it, but I do think Michael limps less now. Maybe he just hides the pain better in the day. He was most jovial today, being Wednesday, when we had two workers – Samson and Prosper – up from the fields to dig over our big patch of weeds. In spring we are to plant it up with vegetables for the house. Fruit too, if I have any say, which I will have if I am still here, and I think, if I'm being honest with myself, I will be.

I made broth for us all, field workers too. Comfort said the workers would not want to come into the house to eat and that I was not to insist on this, or even ask them to as it would make them very uncomfortable. So they had their broth outside by the newly dug ground, standing there dipping their bread into it, and Michael went and stood with them, eating his meal right there too, stick leant against his hip. Comfort did not approve of this. He said it would make the master tired and the workers uncomfortable, again, but they all looked happy enough to me. Three young mannies talking and laughing together under the sun.

I think the sun does Michael good too. But I don't say it. I don't need to criticise Comfort's care of his charge any more than I already have done.

So the weeks go by. I visit the church to take confession, because, with all that has happened, I really need to. The Priest tells me I had no intent to harm anyone, and how that makes a difference. My actions were borne from misfortune alone and, hearing him put it like that does ease my heart a wee bitty. I write more letters. Mr Franklin takes them in. He prints more notices and distributes them too. I see some displayed in shop windows when I visit the city. But there has been no word from Peter, not even a sighting of him. This frustrates me something sare. Sometimes I canna get to sleep for thinking about it. How can no one at all have seen him? I've not even caught sight of someone who looks like him, or heard a Scottish accent while I'm out and about. It's as if my dear love vanished into nothingness the minute he walked away from me and turned that corner.

Obviously there has been no word from Scotland which frustrates me too, but it is more expected and explainable. That was always going to take more than weeks.

When I wake in the night to hammering on the door of the house, my first thought is of Scotland though. I think it is my father dead. I don't know why that is the thought, but it is and it is dreadful. But the truth is dreadful too. Too dreadful. It is one of the field workers at the door, the one called Samson, who smiled at me as he handed his broth bowl back the other day, after the gardening. He is not smiling now. He is frantic.

"The Fo'man is back! The Fo'man is back! He say he going to tear Nivvie's babe from her belly and take it for his own slave to serve him in his house!"

Chapter Twenty-nine

It is gun time. If ever it was gun time, it is now. I ken the house has one, and I ken where it is. I shout to Michael and Comfort as I run to get the great big old gun. The ammunition is in the closet with it and I load it up, thankful that my father taught me about weapons when I was younger. This was probably nae what he had in mind at the time about why I might need the skill – I imagine the Stuart cause was in his thoughts, even back then – but knowledge transfers as it is needed. Comfort and Samson get the horse round and attached to the cart, Michael and Bear climb in, and we're off. Michael has prepared a lamp which is good, because winter is in the air and the night is dark as can be.

Samson tells us what little more he knows as we go. The Fo'man had Nivvie outside and he had a great big knife. Men were gathered and fighting the Fo'man off, though. I hope no one is hurt. I pray no one is hurt. I hold the gun tighter. I hope it is not so old as to not work. Or to backfire. I remember my father's words about that risk. And I've never used a weapon exactly like this. Nothing like as big and heavy as this.

Michael is driving the horse fast so we are there very quickly, and the whole place is in such an uproar of folks running about, it is at first difficult to find Nivvie and the Fo'man. But we soon see them, as they're at the centre of everything, near the cook house.

Nivvie, standing there brave as anything, is screaming curses at Henderson. Samson jumps down from the cart and runs to join her, trying to put himself between her and the Fo'man. A group of men are restraining the evil man himself, but he is hitting and kicking and biting at them, hissing like a caged animal and I know his desperation will cause him to break free soon. His knife keeps missing its many intended marks on my friend, but how long before someone has a finger or a hand severed?

I point the gun right up into the air at an angle, so as to avoid being hit in the face should it misfire, and I pull the trigger. The blast near dislocates my shoulder, but it shoots straight and no one is hit. It certainly gets everyone's attention; they all stop what they are doing and look round at this new terror. Which maybe is not the best thing, for Henderson breaks free, and all in a second he has punched Samson in the face and leapt onto Nivvie, sitting on her, having knocked her to the ground. He rips her dress open, and his knife flashes in the light of torches and lanterns and I don't know where to shoot! I don't know where to aim. I might hit Nivvie. I might hit Samson as he tries to pull Henderson off. Their arms and legs are all confused together in my line of sight.

We are down off the cart. We are running. Bear is at my side, and suddenly I know I have the one weapon that won't miss. "Get him, Bear!" I shout.

Bear is on Fo'man. The man slashes at the dog with the knife. He misses. Bear has him by the throat, right down on the ground, like Fo'man had Nivvie only seconds ago. Bear shakes him by the throat, back and forth, back and forth, so quick like. It is so quick. Fo'man is still. I call Bear back and he comes to stand by me, his mouth a mess of blood. I look back at Fo'man, and know that he is gone. Dead.

It is quiet here in the village. Stars above. A crescent moon. A peaceful night time scene. Till someone, I don't know who, a woman, a child, starts crying. It's not Nivvie because I am looking at her and she is not crying. Comfort rushes – and I do mean rushes – forward to help Samson lift her up from the ground where she still is. She takes two or three steps forward and spits on the body of Henderson.

"I tell you this," says Comfort, still holding Nivvie's hand. "We needs to do something, and we needs to do it fast, or some black necks are gonna be broken for this before long."

"But it was Bear," I say walking forward with the dog. "No man killed anyone."

Comfort nods. "You shot a gun. The dog ripped the throat. But these men here, they fought back against him. This girl here, she fought back against him. You may all be done for it. Women, black men and the dog. A white man dies; somebody is gonna hang."

"He's right," says Rebecca, coming forward and wrapping her arms round Nivvie. "Comfort and me's been alive long enough to know these things."

"No one is going to hang." It's Michael. Stepped to the front to take charge. "There has been a mess made and we're going to clean it up and not speak of it past this night. Anyone who doesn't want to see can go home now. Rebecca, Beth, Nivvie, go to the cook house. Take Bear with you."

Michael, who usually shakes when standing or walking for too long, is solid like a statue. I am the one who feels shaky. I am so worried for us all. What if someone speaks? The white indentured servants? They seem most likely to bring more trouble here.

One of them, a thin sour looking man, speaks now. "You can't put the dog back there with the women. It was the Fo'man's dog and it needs putting down."

Rage quells my shakes. "He was protecting Nivvie. He was protecting us all."

"Aye," says Michael, and it's strange to hear him speaking my language. "The dog was not Henderson's; he was mine, of this plantation, his job to protect us from attackers and that's what he's done tonight. But he's Miss Beth's dog now. He's devoted to her. And I know he won't hurt a one of you unless there is violence that needs to be stopped."

And that's it. No one questions him. And no one stops us taking Bear with us to the cook house. No one mentions that it was me who set Bear on a man. Or that the man died because of my action. I start to shake a wee bitty again. Because this is not the first time my choices have led to a death. I need to face it: this is not the first time I have... killed. I stop and look up at the stars again, feeling so cold, and so shocked, by what's happened, and by myself.

"Come on, Miss Beth," says Nivvie. "It'll be all right in the end."

I shake off the cold thoughts, for surely it should not be Nivvie comforting me at this point. She is the one who was attacked. She is the one who is very heavily with child now. So, arms round each other, we three lassies make our way to the cook house with no more delay.

"Rebecca, he's coming," says Nivvie as soon as we're through the door, and at first I think she means the Fo'man and that she is feeling frightened and confused like me after all that's happened this night. But, no. She means her baby. That's who's coming.

So as one body is put quietly and secretly down into the earth, another comes into this world. He arrives quickly and easily, so says Rebecca, though it seems a terrible process to me. The tiny boy starts shouting and crying as soon as he's born, loud as can be, so maybe he didna much like the process either. Nivviee doesn't want to take him from Rebecca. She doesn't want to look on his face, so Rebecca hands him to me, and I sit by Nivvie on the cot, holding the wee bundle of blanket and babe.

"He reminds me of my brother," I say. "He looked like this when he was born. All pink and wrinkled. But he soon grew. And smoothed out, like. His eyes changed from blue to brown. And he was my favourite person in the whole world."

"What was his name?" asks wee Mary, having been awoken by the birth, and thankfully not what came before.

"Thomas. It's a family name. My Grandfather, the bear, he was called Thomas too."

The new baby fusses and reaches out his arms. I turn him towards Nivvie, sad that she doesn't want him, but understanding the whys of it.

"He knows you not his Mama," says Rebecca to me.

"Course he knows," says Nivvie, sitting up and seeming to shake off her sad state. "Give him here. Give Lil Thomas to me."

By the time the men show up, Lil Thomas has a full belly of milk and a full name: Thomas Samson Comfort Michael, called for my wee brother and the good men who were nearby when he was born. Of bad men, none of us say a thing.

Chapter Thirty

The year turns fully into winter, covering the ground in thick fluffy snow. Well it looks fluffy until you walk into it. Then it's just the same as the snow I knew in Scotland, deep and cold and soaking the clothes right through. Also the same as in Scotland, is the lack of fresh food. But I learn to make many tasty dishes with the ingredients I have to hand: wee fried cakes of ground beans and spices, stews, pies, soups. We do not go hungry. Not a one of us.

No one comes looking for the Fo'man. No one at all. It is almost unbelievable, or like a miracle. I wake often in the night, thinking I've heard a banging at the door, and then feel most affa sad, because what if I were to be sent to the gallows before I've had a chance to find Peter, or return to Scotland? I feel strange when in town too and I see Red Coats, government troops as we called them at home. They would do something about what I did with that gun, and my dog, if they knew, I'm sure.

But no one at all comes looking for Elizabeth Manteith of the castle. I'm not so stupid to think a letter from me could have reached Scotland and one come back yet, but somewhere in the back parts of my mind I must have been fostering a vain hope that maybe someone would have found out what happened to me, and someone would have followed.

And who knows? Maybe I am being looked for just as I am looking for Peter. In all the wrong places. Maybe the Fo'man's killer is being looked for in those places too. Or maybe he was as horrible and vile as he was here to most everybody, so no one much cares that he is missing.

I eat turkey for the first time at Christmas. The whole plantation eats it. Well, not Lil Thomas, he just has his mama's milk. But that little boy, he knows me. He smiles when he sees me, and it does make my heart squeeze a wee bit. I am his Auntie Beth. How old that does make me sound, and in truth I am older than my years, with all that has happened. I found a mirror, in the back of the pantry of all places, and after the horror of the mess of my mad hair, I saw that I was older, fair grown up looking in fact.

So 1743, the year that I arrived in America, comes to an end, and it is now 1744. And I am still here.

Winter is long and cold and dark, but the fire inside is warm and bright. Michael and Comfort and me often sit in the kitchen together now. To eat and to talk and to plan. We make plans as if I will still be here, and we make plans to make sure I get home. Vegetable planting and letters. More ideas of people to ask about Peter.

The Laudanum is finished with now, replaced with chocolate and friends. We dwell on how a bottle of drops can so change and ruin a life.

"It is not the drops as does that," says Comfort. "It is the sadness that comes before the drops."

Comfort is a much happier man now. We tease him about his visits to the cook house and Rebecca. After the night that no one speaks of, Comfort has been accepted back into the fold down there, whatever bad feelings existed blasted away with the firing of a gun. Or that's how I think of it.

And when loud banging on the door in the middle of the night really does happen again? It is not Scotland I think of first. It's Michael, and then Comfort. Because, what has happened? Are they ill? Or hurt? Shot or bit? Are we found out? Are our necks to be broken for the Fo'man?

But it is nothing to do with any of that at all. It is Hannah at the back door of the kitchen, Hannah who tells me with some words and more gestures that I have to go into the trees with her to help Eliza. I know what is happening. I think I do anyway.

I shout to Michael and Comfort, asking then to build up the fire and go down to the village and get Rebecca or someone, anyone, who can help with the birthing of a baby.

I know as soon as I see Eliza that this will not be the same 'quick and easy' process that it was for Nivvie. There is dark blood on the snow where she crouches, and her screams echo between the tall trees. But we get her back up to the house, Hannah and me. Michael throws his stick to the side and carries her for the last bit of the way when he sees us coming.

Rebecca and Nivvie and Mary and Lil Thomas all arrive at the house to help. The three male persons among us, Lil Thomas being one of them and fast asleep, are chased away to the back room by Rebecca, and we try to settle Eliza in front of the fire, for she is most affa cold. But she is for wandering all over the house crying. She likes Bear, she wants to sit with him. Then she wants Hannah. Then she wants me. Then she just cries and sobs, kneeling in the middle of the kitchen floor, and wants no one.

"Who is this child, come straight out of the night like this, Beth?" asks Rebecca, accusation in her tone.

"She is a friend of mine," I explain. "The quines helped me when I was first here, in this land. In fact, I would probably not be living now if it were not for their help."

Rebecca nods as Eliza's screams start again with a new depth and anguish to them like I've never heard before. It takes me back to the ship when we thought we were all to die, but it is not the same, not quite the same. But risk of death is near. For someone. I can feel it. And I can hear it.

I make chocolate. Rebecca agrees. We have to try something to alter Eliza's spirits. But the chocolate makes her sick. So then, feeling sick about it myself, I ask Michael if he has any drops left. And he does. He wants to take the cart to Philadelphia to fetch a doctor.

"There is no time for that," says Rebecca. "What's happening here is going to happen quick from now, one way or the other. The poppy will lessen the pain."

I don't know if it does; I hope it does. Mayhaps it would be worse without it, but I can't see how. Eliza screams like she is being sawn in two. We have her in front of the fire now, squatting, because the bairn is nearly here, but it takes all four of us, Rebecca, Nivvie, Hannah and me, to stop her from running off into the woods again for that's where she wants to go.

Rebecca slaps Eliza's face. "You gonna push this child out of you and be done with it. There is no running off from this!"

The baby is not born crying and screaming. She is quiet. And so still. Rebecca pats her back and gives her a good rubbing and clears her throat and nose of gunge, but the baby stays still. Eliza doesn't care. She curls up in a ball by the fire, her head in Hannah's lap. She takes chocolate now. She drinks it up.

But I can't stop looking at the tiny wee baby girl. She is so beautiful. And so perfect. All her fingers and toes, so dainty, so sweet. I take a blanket and wrap her round.

"Maybe take her out of the room," suggests Rebecca, who I think is relieved that Eliza has calmed down. "Sometimes it's better for the mother not to see it."

It. Death. Like Thomas. My first wee Thomas. No. I won't accept it. I wrap the baby more tightly and take her out of the room. I take her through to show Michael and Comfort.

"Born sleeping," says Comfort, nodding.

"Aye," I say, able to accept sleeping over death. I walk all round the house, singing to the baby. I go upstairs and take her into Michael's room and sit with her there on the bed for a bit, rocking to and fro, to and fro. It really is a very nice room. With many book shelves and books. We take a turn in Comfort's room too, and it is also a pleasant place. It has a window seat and I think it probably lets in sunlight during the day. I sing all the lullabies I can remember from childhood, sitting there, and then, realising this is not what I should be doing, I sing jollier songs. Ballads from the times gone by. Scottish lassies and laddies longing for each other across the sea. And I dance. Down the stairs. Up the stairs. Round and round my own room and right through into the room where the mannies are.

For a moment I think Lil Thomas has started to cry. But it is not him. The babe in my arms, the newest quine among us, has awakened.

Chapter Thirty-one

Eliza takes her baby like there was never any problem, and puts her to the breast. Nivvie puts a cup of chocolate in my hand and I am right glad of it. Because I have come over a bit shaky now, thinking about all that has happened this night, in fact both these nights of babes being born are sitting with me here in front of the fireplace.

But all is good now. All is peaceful and well. We are a family of women round this big roaring fire with our big roaring Bear to guard us. Not that he's roaring now. He's quiet and calm, as I am starting to be too.

I lay my head down beside my dog on the rug and drift off into a dream of wee babies, maybe my own wee babies, only to be awakened to actual angry roaring. It is Rebecca and she is furious. Michael and Comfort are through here now too, perhaps summoned by the noise. It seems Eliza has announced her intention of heading back out into the snowy woods with her new daughter and Hannah.

Rebecca is shouting about the baby having been born dead. Eliza didn't know that and she is crying.

"But even if she had come out wailing, you cannot live in the woods with a new-born infant."

Rebecca's right. I know she's right. But Eliza is afraid of something, and I'm sure she's right to be too.

"No one comes out here in winter," I tell her. "Could you not stay for now? You could stay hidden in the house with us. Who would know?"

"You listen to Miss Beth," says Rebecca. "She the one brought that child back from heaven for you. She won't let no danger come to her."

I can see Eliza thinking, looking down at her daughter.

"Stay here for now," urges Michael. "Then, could we not have bought new slaves?"

We all look at him. I, at least, am horrified.

"You need to stay hidden," he says, having picked up on that. "There are empty quarters down at the village. You could stay there, join in whatever work you wish when you are able. No one is to know you are not owned. You can leave at any point of course," he adds.

So that is what happens. The quines stay. First in our house. And then, once it has been made ready, Hannah and Eliza and the wee babe move down to their own hoosie in the village.

Eliza calls her baby Bethany. I think Rebecca had a say in that, because it is her who explains the meaning of the name. "Bethany is a village in the bible. Our Lord visited Martha and Mary and Lazarus there. And he did raise Lazarus from the dead. And your name is right there in the place Miss Beth."

I am now called to all birthings that happen in the village. I am happy enough to go along, but worried that people think my presence is some sort of assurance of things going well. I always take chocolate and have the dark drops in my pocket too, just in case. But so far, I've never had to use them. My grandmother from long ago did midwifing. I tell the story of The Mermaid and the Bear to the labouring women. I don't know if it helps, if it takes their mind off their pain for a minty, but I hope it does.

The snow finally melts. And the sun comes back out, all warm and happy for spring. I feel excitement in my belly. For enough time has passed now that a letter could come from Scotland. Or even a person might arrive.

I keep myself busy though. I take the old horse, who soon starts to feel like my horse, and ride out into the wilder and more remote parts of the country to enquire at farms about Peter, but this proves no more fruitful than our previous methods. I plant up a vegetable garden by the house, with help from Eliza and Hannah, wee Bethany tied to our backs by turns. I enjoy seeing the house being painted and looking all new again. The shutters are right bonny things, very useful too. We put seats out on the porch, and as the evenings get lighter Michael, Comfort and I often sit out to drink tea or chocolate.

The tobacco is planted and growing now. May 12th comes and goes and it is now one year since I was taken from Scotland, and no word has come.

I still write letters every month, sending one to each of the Manteith family properties and extra ones to other relatives, some so distant they maybe won't remember who I am, and maybe I've not got their house names quite right, but if there's even the smallest chance of something helping in my quest to get home, I'm going to do it.

I still do everything I can think of to find Peter too, and pray that I find him in good time for us to travel back to Scotland together. I put more notices in different shops and taverns. I ride out to more and more farms and plantations. But, as the tobacco plants grow taller and taller, an uneasy feeling is growing in me, a feeling that it all is for naught. That maybe I should just accept my lot and keep cooking. And cleaning. And sweeping the porch. And that I will never see my home, or my true love again.

Lil Thomas and Bethany giggle and laugh together; one can crawl, the other can roll, and they do get into some mischief. They are like brother and sister, those two. Rebecca and Eliza often fight, shouting and screaming about one thing or another, often what is right to do with Bethany, feeding-wise, clothing-wise… They are like mother and daughter, those two. So says Nivvie. Hannah is still quiet. But I can tell that she's happy living with Eliza in their wee house in the back of the plantation. They are a happy wee family.

Mrs Sour approaches our house in the full swelter of summer as I am outside wiping down the windows. I keep them spotless now, all shiny and bright, so I can see everything, and anyone, that is coming to visit.

"Set up the parlour, girl," she says to me. "You have fine company this afternoon."

I look round, heart all thumping like. Who has come? And from where?

I know as soon as I see the fine lady in her hooped dress and fancy hat that she is neither from Scotland, nor here for me in any way. She's tiptoeing around the muddier bits on the ground; this is not someone who has just endured a long sea journey.

Mrs Sour hisses at me to make sure Michael is looking his best, and as this only confirms that the visitor is not for me, I ignore the nasty old woman, push my hair out of my face and carry on cleaning my windows. I am not her servant to order about.

Chapter Thirty-two

I soon have to come down from my ladder and enter the house, for Mrs Sour and the fine lady are in my kitchen looking at everything and saying how things could be better arranged. And cleaner. The sheer and utter cheek of them.

"How can I help you?" I say, as I go in, making clear, I hope, that this is my domain.

"We will take tea in the parlour," says Mrs Sour, and both ladies swish past me in their finery.

I, in direct contrast, am in my oldest dress, the one the slavers bought me, to save spoiling my other clothes while cleaning. I briefly consider going to change, maybe even putting on my best flowery gown. But what is the point? What is the point of any of it? I bang and crash pots around in my annoyance as I get ready tea things on a tray. Then I notice Sarah, sitting outside in the waggon, holding the reins of the horse. I knock on the window and beckon to her, but she shakes her head.

Out I go.

A short conversation with Sarah does not improve my mood. She has been ordered most sternly to remain outside so that Mrs Sour can leave without any notice. She is on no account to enter the house to visit with her brother. Well!

Michael comes through, just as I am re-entering the house. "Rachel would like to try some chocolate if that's all right, Beth. What a surprise this is. One of my childhood friends come to visit." Off back through he goes to the visitors, face full of smiles. Well!

Comfort comes through to join me in the kitchen. Comfort stays through. Of course he does.

"That's us shown our place now," I say to him. "Servants through here in the kitchen. And out there in the waggon."

He looks confused, as if he doesn't see the problem. I'm too annoyed to explain and, in truth, my thoughts feel a bit all over the place anyway. But I prepare drinks and food for Comfort and Sarah and myself, just as good as theirs. Actually better. For a devilish thought comes over me, and I follow it through. I prepare chocolate for Michael, Comfort, Sarah and myself in the usual way. With sugar. I make a special cup for Rachel, beautiful Rachel with her fine dress and her haughty ways. With salt. I'm sure she wouldn't want sugar anyway.

Comfort watches me slice up the raisin cake. I plop a tray in front of him.

"There's both tea and chocolate there for Sarah to try if she pleases. You take it out to her and I'll take theirs through. There's a cup for you too."

"Thank you kindly, Miss Beth," he says, a small smile on his face. I think he finds my anger amusing.

So now it's time for me to go through to the parlour. I lay down the tray of the second best china upon the table in the middle of the room. The first best is out at the waggon. And I pass the chocolate cups to Michael and Rachel, making sure to give them the right ones. Rachel thanks me and smiles prettily from under her smooth golden hair. I prepare Mrs Sour's black tea in the meticulous way she requests, and then I leave, not speaking a word in any of my time there. I do not curtsey. I will not curtsey.

I continue to bang around the kitchen, tidying up the pots until Comfort comes back in. "Sit down, quine," he says.

So I do. More with the shock of him calling me a quine than anything else, I think.

"I'm learning some of your Scottish words," he says.

I've learned too and instead of 'aye', I say: "For sure you are, Comfort, for sure you are."

"They won't be staying long," he says. "We'll be back to ourselves soon."

But we won't. I know, I mean of course I've always actually known, that I am a servant in this house. Until such time as I can get home to Scotland, I have a position here. One of servitude. Paid servitude. I am luckier than many. And I ken I'm probably spoilt for this, but I dinna feel lucky in this moment. I am all a-churn with something poisonous. And I'm hoping that Miss Rachel is choking on her salty cup of chocolate. Choking and spluttering the staining brown drink all over her fine dress.

She does not choke on it. She declares it, "A most interesting beverage," when she comes through to look down upon us in the kitchen before leaving.

"Michael tells me you are from the Aberdeen area of Scotland," she says, and I nod. "I have relatives there," she says, and she tells me their name. I recognise it. Aberdeen merchants. A family much below my own. And one that Peter named as being involved in the kidnap of many innocents from the quayside at Aberdeen. So I say nothing, just nod again, when she says she will write to them on my behalf, for what good will that do?

They go, Mrs Sour and Rachel and Sarah. Back to Philadelphia.

"Had you heard of Rachel's family?" asks Michael after going out to say, and who knows, maybe to kiss, goodbye to the visitors.

"Aberdeen merchants who profit from the kidnapping and sale of children," I tell him.

"No!" says Michael, all shocked like.

"Aye!" I say back in the same tone.

"Are you sure, Beth? How do you know this?"

"Peter told me."

Michael frowns and I can see it does not suit him to believe this information. So he chooses not to. "Peter and you were little more than children when you were taken. I'm sure Rachel's family were not involved. How can you really know that?"

I am so incensed, there are no words to express it. "Fitever you say, sir," I say to him, not looking at him, and I pick up my food basket and walk out of the back door, and head to the cook house.

Chapter Thirty-three

By the time I reach the village my rage has grown. I feel it growing in me like a disease. My mind is full of Michael's handsome face. Rachel's beautiful one. Me in my ragged state of clothing. And then I feel faint. And then a terrible pain passes across my belly, just before everything goes purple and black with wee specks of yellow. And then just dark.

When I wake I am in the cook house, lying on the bunk at the side. I'm still in pain but the rage has dissipated.

"You've got your courses, Miss Beth," says Nivvie, from where she sits beside me. "Do you always faint with them?"

"My courses?" Courses. Monthlies. I haven't had them for so long. Not since before the ship. Probably the near starvation stopped them then, and now that I am more settled they have begun again. I curl up on the bunk, eyes closed, trying to fight the need to cry like a wee bairn. Because, I am not more settled. I'm a servant. I canna bear to think about Michael and Rachel and how he just spoke to me about Peter, and I dinna ken fit to do now.

"I thinks maybe you should stay here today," says Rebecca, coming over to look at me. "Nivvie could go and make your mannies' supper. Do you think the master would accept that? We will say you're not well."

I'm not sure what he'll think about it but Nivvie goes anyway and doesn't come back, so he must have accepted it. Which is just as well, as I don't want to go back to the house. Not yet. Actually not ever. But I know that's stupid. I want to stay here with Rebecca, I feel right here. The house isn't the same anymore. Something changed this afternoon. And I just want to stay here.

So I do. Day after day, Nivvie sets off every morning and comes back in the evening. She likes it, working in the house, being in charge of the kitchen. "Even that Comfort is all right to work with," she says. "Though they is both worried about you. The master wants to come and see you."

"No!" I really do not want that.

All I want is to help with the preparations of the food and sit with the babies. I just love them. They haven't learned any of the nonsense of the world yet. They don't see rich or poor, free or owned, black or white. They see if we're smiley and nice to play with, or if we're grumpy and to be ignored, like some of the less nice workers down here are. And those babies love me right back. Bethany is sitting up now and Lil Thomas crawls round and round us both at great speed. He's happy to stay with me while Nivvie goes to the house sometimes, though he goes there with her too some days.

I don't go to church that week, or the next. Still I am here in the cook house. All alone on a Sunday. I decide to get up, to walk about the village in its emptiness. And who comes bounding up, but Bear? He must have got out of the house when everyone left. My, I've missed him. I've regretted not taking my dog with me on more than one occasion, and I kneel down to hug him properly now. But Bear has betrayed me. He has not come alone.

I hear Michael's voice calling my name, but I hesitate to react, to turn and see him, for I feel strange and I just keep my eyes on Bear, my hands rubbing his fur. I feel a bit silly for flouncing off like I did, and also for never going back. I feel embarrassed by it all. I don't want to explain about my courses. Not to a man. But I am glad that Nivvie bullied me into putting on my finest gown for Sunday, even though I wasn't going out. She brought it down from the house with her yesterday. Nivvie! She knew he was going to come here today. Oh, the double betrayal.

Michael doesn't ask me any of the whys of anything. He just says, "I've missed you, Beth. Will you not come back?"

"Nivvie is a good cook," I say, still facing Bear, the sulky feeling creeping back in as I talk.

"Aye, she is," he says, the bare faced cheek of him using my language like that. And then, the sheer audacity: "Maybe even better than you."

I stand up slowly and turn to look him right in the face. He's not smiling, not joking with me. He says, "It's you I miss, Beth." And he looks so sad that I want to hug him. But I don't. He goes on, "I know you've been sad. And I don't know how to help you with that. But it will come. You will go home. These things take time, is all."

This is not what made me sad, but it should have been. My priorities have become so confused and muddled here. And that needs to stop, right now. Rachel shouldn't bother me. Michael shouldn't bother me, not even as I look at his face, all full of concern and kindness. My heart should be filled with home. And Peter. And, of course, it is.

So we walk back to the house, Michael and Bear and I.

"You should have taken the cart," I say.

"It's gone with everyone to town."

"Sometimes I think there's not much wrong with your leg." The words are out of my mouth before I think to stop them. But I don't really care. It's a day of truthful talking.

"There isn't," he says. "Doctors say there's nothing wrong with it."

I look at him, astonished by this. I mean, I knew he could throw his stick to the side and walk and even run on it if need be, but nothing wrong at all?

"It's been this way since my father died. We were out in the waggon, and he let me take the reins, let me drive the horse. Something frightened it in the woods, it reared and the cart tipped. My father was crushed, he was dead at once. My leg was trapped. And it's never worked right since."

"Oh, Michael," I say and stop. There's a forced steadiness to his voice that lets me know he doesn't want sympathy. But I can picture the scene, the young bairn, with his father lying there dead. And I need to know more, to understand properly. "How long till help came?"

"Two days." He says it matter of factly, no emotion about him at all.

I take his hand and we walk the rest of the way home like that together.

And the very next day? A letter comes from Scotland.

Chapter Thirty-four

It's not from my father. I ken that as soon as I look at it, by the writing on the front. The wax seal is stamped with the Manteith family crest, the Mermaid and the Bear and the heart. So it is from home. It is from the castle.

It's from Eppy. Bless her, her writing is not very good, but I understand at once that she is saying things in between the words that she has written. She's right glad I'm alive and well. And she's right glad I'm safe. Many folks are now fearing they winna be, not for long. My mother is well. My father is well. Jock is well. He has a new companion to keep him company as he goes about his rounds, a wee dog he did find on the quayside in Aberdeen. A spaniel! I'm so overjoyed and relieved to hear this part that I get up and hug Michael and Comfort, explaining all about Prince Charles to them, before wiping my eyes and reading on. My father is busy, so busy, busy, busy, and moving around all the time, a difficult man to find. But I should keep writing to the different properties; a letter is bound to reach him at some point.

But for now, Eppy tells me, I am as well to be safe on the other side of the sea. And then, doon by her name, there's wee drawing, a doodle. Beside it she's written: 'A white rose for you, from the bonny rose garden this year.' There is no rose garden at the castle. I hold the picture near to my face and see that in the centre of the rose is the word 'FIAT'.

And I understand.

"Fiat means 'Let it come to pass,'" I explain to Michael and Comfort who seem to think the letter odd. "The white rose is a Jacobite symbol. Rebellion is at hand."

"Rebellion?" says Michael. "Or outright war? She must think truly terrible things are to come if she's advising you to stay here and be safe.

Myself too, I am glad you're to be safe here. Your father won't send for you until things are settled, I'm sure."

"Aye, you're gonna have to put up with me a wee minty more, boys!" I say, full of bravado on the outside, though I do feel a bit like crying on the inside, partly for the disappointment that this letter was not arranging a return to Scotland. But also because, though Eppy is right to say that I am safe, what about her and Jock and my father? How long will they be safe? Redcoats were already patrolling our lands before I left home. Already suspicious of the Manteith family's loyalties.

The wee minty stretches as I long for more news of home. I ask everyone if they have heard anything about what is going on in England and Scotland and with the king. I ask Mr Franklin. I ask my fellow worshippers at church. I even ask the beautiful and refined Rachel when we run into her in Philadelphia one Sunday, though she has no information. I don't think she ever wrote to her relatives about me, else she would mention it now. She's more interested in asking Michael how it goes at the plantation, how profits are, and I suspect her priorities of being just like those of her Aberdeen family. He doesn't tell her much, or try to extend our meeting with her, and for that I am glad.

So no one has heard anything. But, even though there is never any news, I keep on asking about the two things that matter the most. For news of Scotland. And news of Peter.

My birthday rolls round again and this time I ken fit date it is and I let everyone else ken about it too. We have a wee feast down at the village. My 'wee minty' in America is broken up with wee feasts and celebrations and church and weekly meetings.

Mr Lay comes to visit as late in the autumn. He has heard that there is much unrest in Scotland. And much oppression. Aye well, I already kent that. But it is good of him to visit me. Though he is difficult to feed. He doesn't take sugar, due to its being produced by slaves. He tells me a terrible tale of a boy being burnt alive in the giant pot used to refine the sugar. He won't take chocolate, because he doesn't know if slavery is involved in its production. He has a mint tea made from mint I grew myself beside the house, and I do him a plate of fruit grown here too.

Mr Lay approves of my vegetable garden, and I give him some bits to take home. He is surprised that I grow squash and corn.

"That was Hannah's idea," I tell him. "They grow so well here, as do…" I wander along and point at one of my best crops: "Beans!"

"And you have young Michael growing tall and strong as a beanstalk too," he says, as Michael comes out of the house.

"Don't trust this man," says Michael, then repeating the words. "Do not trust this man." But I can tell from his grin and obvious fondness of Mr Lay that he does not mean it. He is speaking in jest only. "He kidnapped me once, you know Beth," he says and I think he must be making that up, but no… Michael was the wee loon that Mr Lay took to show what it is to lose a child to kidnapping and slavery.

"The joke was on you, Mr Lay," he says. "My mother was sorely disappointed to get me back!" And, sadly, though it is said in good humour, I do not think this is a joke.

"Your father was so relieved, he wept," Mr Lay tells him. "He would be glad to see you back out in the world."

Back out in the world Michael is, busily overseeing the harvesting of the tobacco. "This is set to be our most profitable year yet," he tells us at the weekly meeting. "And with no brutality and no hunger. It gives me hope that this plantation can be managed without slavery one day."

This does cause an awful to-do and panic in the room. People are worried about what that means? Will they be thrown out of their homes? Apparently there are stories of that happening to freed slaves who then can't get work and just starve.

"I will never throw anyone out," says Michael. "Whether I can afford to pay you a decent wage is another matter. However, I do not own the plantation. These are matters for far into the future. Who knows what will change between then and now?"

"Aye, evil takes its time in dying," whispers Comfort to me and I look at him, shocked. It's the first time I've heard him speak up and out against anything, or anyone.

I smile at him and say: "For sure."

Chapter Thirty-five

And just as evil people take their time dying, evil acts take their time being undone. What was done to Peter and myself goes on unhindered by my efforts to end it. We are still here. Still lost to each other and Scotland. And there is no sign of any change to this situation.

Time goes on. Life goes on.

The wee bairns, or babies as we all still call Bethany and Lil Thomas, mirror that passage of time as they grow. Truly there is not much difference in them from day to day, but soon they are walking, and talking, and learning to be cheeky, and great change has taken place without any of us seeing how it happened. I hope other changes are like this too, such as important letters, as yet unseen, already crossing the sea to me. Peter might be, at this very moment, planning to walk down a street at the same time as I am there. Anything could happen at any time and I must stay alert and ready for it.

And my wee minty in America continues to be broken up by wee golden minties of its own. I see the first frost of winter lit up by the early morning sun through my big kitchen windows. Then snow. Then the first shoots of spring. The crops grow. They are harvested. I cook. I clean. I smile and laugh with Comfort and Michael and Nivvie and Rebecca and Wee Mary. I enjoy many happy visits with the quines in their wee hoosie. And it makes the time seem less. In truth I do not often stop to think about how long I have been here. Because it's now years. And it could seem like never ending years, and that's an upsetting thought and it won't help me get home any quicker. I do note the dates as I write to Eppy and my father. I see the numbers written there at the top of the paper, not to be ignored. And as 1744 becomes last year, not this year anymore, I smile at Eppy's tale of Prince Charles chasing rabbits through the kitchen garden and flattening all the herbs in the process, square my shoulders, and go on.

The biggest celebration, or golden mintie, happens in autumn of 1745, late on, but before the cold of winter sets in. And it is, deservedly, a very great celebration indeed: Nivvie's wedding.

She 'jumps the broom' with Samson, who I knew she had become close with. The festivities are merry in the extreme, the best we've had so far, for there is both dancing and music, late into the night.

"We need to find a nice white boy for you to be a marrying," Nivvie says to me halfway through the revelries. "So's you can get a baby of your own. You love the babies." I think she has had quite a fill of the strong wine Michael ordered for the occasion.

"What if I don't want a nice white boy?" I answer back, loud in my defiance, also having had a fair fill of the wine.

"Has to be a white boy," says Nivvie. "Nothing else allowed."

"Really?" I say, saddened by such nonsense, but then not wanting to bring the happy mood down, I add, "But what if I want to marry Comfort?" And that does cause much mirth around us.

"I think there is probably better candidates," says Comfort.

"Yes!" says Nivvie. "We have to find Miss Beth's Peter for her. Her true love and the most bravest and handsomest Scotsman in all the world."

Rebecca joins in, "So they can live in the most beautiful castle in all the world."

I find myself flushing, face all hot and not just from the wine. It's a confusing feeling. I do long to find Peter of course, and I know he is my true love, but in truth I have not been thinking of him in a romantic sort of way for a while. The suggestion that I would marry him feels odd. I am older now than when we separated, and realise: how can I even know that he would want such a thing? Nivvie and Samson know each other so well and they have made this decision based on their ongoing friendship and love. Peter and I haven't seen one another for over two years. We were abducted captives together. Terrified captives. That's why we held hands in the street on that last day. How could we have known if there was more to it, or not? Or not. Doubt has most definitely crept in. About the true love stuff. What if it was all nonsense? Just a silly wee lassie with silly wee ideas in her mind? But, no. I shake my head to clear it of the nasty thought. And I remember the gingerbread that Peter brought me when I was locked up all alone, and how good it tasted, and how kind it was of him.

"Look, you gone and made Miss Beth all sad," says Samson. "I know what'll fix her. A dance with me!"

I don't know if it fixes me. I am all dizzied up after it. But I'm real happy for Nivvie. Samson was a good dancing partner, very considerate and not too rough. It's been a long time since I danced with a man; years and years, but I remember it being too violent and fast sometimes. And if he's a good dancing partner, he'll be a good husband, surely? And I find myself flushing again, all over this time.

I sit down beside Michael, who I think has not indulged as heavily in the wine as the rest of us. He is quieter, any road. I want to ask him to dance. I think he could. But he might not want to. And it might be unpleasant or painful for him. I feel all confused and flushed, yet again.

"You like dancing, Beth," he says.

It wasn't a question but I nod. "I've had enough of it for tonight though, I think," I tell him. "And too much wine."

"It's good to see you look so happy," he says. "It'll make your 'minty' here pass all the quicker."

It does, I think. But it's not till the very end of the year, when the sky is threatening and heavy with snow, that I next hear about Scotland. And it's not a letter this time; it's just news being talked about in Philadelphia. I'm buying special treats at the market for us to have at Christmas when I hear it being said and exclaimed about by two wifies: The Jacobites have marched South. I rush to Mr Franklin's shop, and not just to get chocolate this time. Surely he will know more details. He does, but not many. The Young Pretender, as they're calling Bonnie Prince Charlie, landed in Scotland in the summer. The Jacobite army has taken Edinburgh and defeated the British troops in a battle at Prestonpans.

They're winning! They're actually winning! We could have a new king next year. A rightful king. A Stuart. I quickly realise people hereabouts do not think this will be a good thing. They do not want to have a whole load of new laws foisted upon them by another king in a far off land. I do see their point… But… the Jacobites are winning!

I pray for their safety. I pray that there be as little loss of life and suffering as possible. But I do pray for them to win. And real quick too, so I can go home.

The whole of Christmas feels lit up with excitement this year. Snow all round, babies at the hearth, because our own little 'family' gathers to eat and celebrate together in our house.

Michael gives me a plaid, a bit like the one I lost, though this one is woven through with both green and blue. I have moaned a fair bit about the theft of my plaid. This new one is most affa cosy, and I do feel truly contented here in front of the big fire in the kitchen, with all my friends round me. The babies, or small children as they are now, are fascinated with the plaid and soon we turn the large garment into a tent for them around me and over the chair. I wriggle out to sit free and watch them play.

"Bethany's making camp, look," says Eliza, a wistful tone in her voice, and come spring 1746 that's what they do, Hannah and Eliza and Bethany. They go back into the woods. And there's nothing any the one of us can do about it. They're going to stay with a section of Hannah's people that they feel safe with, some distance away. They say they will visit us again in the future. And I really hope they do. Before I have to leave.

We swap back the Elfin Blade and the leather bracelet. The action brings me no joy. I dinna really want to take the elf arrow back to Scotland. I dinna ken why, but it feels wrong to take ownership of it again, like it's not really mine. It's certainly not a lucky object, and I feel a saddening the moment it is back in my hand. And I liked the leather bracelet. I would rather have kept that.

Lil Thomas is heartbroken with the loss of his friend. He cries and cries for her. I understand. I know how big a wrench this will be for me too when I return to Scotland. As I must. But I will leave bits of my heart scattered all around this house and plantation.

Chapter Thirty-six

Shortly after the quines leave, in April, another letter comes from Eppy. And the news is good. I run all over the house, unable to contain all the exuberance I feel about it. There has been a battle in the general region of the castle, at Inverurie, and the Jacobites won there too. Though Eppy does not outright say this, it's there in the wee tale she tells.

I read it to Comfort and Michael: "You remember the MacCrimmon piper, Elizabeth? The one called Donald? The finest of the Highland pipers, so they say. Well, he was taken prisoner at the Battle of Inverurie this December just gone. And they say all the Jacobite pipers refused to play after that, out of respect for the man, until he was set free. So freed he was and he about turned and went straight back to the Red Coats! What a to-do!"

Eppy goes on to say that she thinks she might be seeing me soon, and that she looks forward to that day dearly.

"They are winning their battles," says Michael, thoughtfully.

"Aye they are." I dance about the kitchen for the joy of it.

"But things can change overnight in war, Beth," adds Michael. "It only takes one loss, one mistake. And many die, whoever wins."

He's right. I know my father might die in this, might already be dead. But I canna think of it. Not properly. Not as anything more than empty words in my head. But I dream of it sometimes at night. Dreadful bloody battles. With screaming. And shooting. And stabbing. All manner of vileness that I have never seen the like of. Well, I have seen beatings and whippings. And I, myself, pushed a man off a ship. I, myself, ordered a dog to end a man's life. But this is more than those sudden and singular deaths. This is a different level of violence, of gore and cutting and hurting and killing.

I have also heard further tales of human cruelty from Mr Lay. Recently he was here again telling of his time in Jamaica where enslaved women were persuaded to bear children for extra food, and even a promise of freedom if they produced many bairns. But it was to swell the ranks of the slave population. They would be freed but have to leave their children behind. It's so horrible I don't want to think of it too deeply either, though the knowledge of it makes me put less sugar in my cooking.

But cook I do. Garden I do. Busy, busy, busy. It takes the edge off the excitement I feel about the Jacobites winning. My vegetables grow so well this year. So does the tobacco. Another bit of profit will be going into Mrs Sour's purse. There is a woman who dampens excitement and happiness wherever she goes. And she does seem to visit us rather a lot of late. Occasionally with Rachel, but most often on her own.

It is a terrible thing to say, but I hate Mrs Sour. She looks at me like I am a piece of dirt on her shoe, but really I am nothing to her, and she is nothing to me, so it does not bother me overly much. It is for the way she treats Michael and Comfort and Sarah that I actually detest her. Comfort and Sarah are brother and sister and fond ones at that. Mrs Sour always has Sarah drive her here and now she always commands her to stay outside with the horse and trap, even in bad weather. What is the point of this meanness? There is none, as Eppy would say, it's 'just for coarseness' or the cruelty of keeping people who love each other apart. Sarah doesn't seem to mind much at all. In fact, when I take her tea out to the cart and express my opinion on the matter, she laughs. "Oh, we have to let her have her fun sometimes," she says.

But then, there's how Mrs Sour treats Michael; if Rachel has not come with her, the old woman spends every minute of her time here telling him how useless he is. Whatever he does is not good enough. Since he took over the running of the plantation properly, it has been more profitable, but the way she goes on? You'd think the opposite was true. Everything he arranges is wrong to her. When we had our house painted and freshened up: it was declared not nearly as good as hers. She had two white mannies in to do it for her. We had workers from the fields. It was a change for them and they made a beautiful job of it. But

Mrs Sour is one of those people who uses the colour of a person's skin to make her feel better about herself. She looks down on those who are different from her. She is more than sour. She is foul.

She is also full of tales of young men, Michael's age, who are getting married and having children; her friends all have grandchildren, but not her, oh no, not her. I'm just amazed she has friends. Maybe they are cut from the same ugly cloth as her.

So perhaps it is fitting that, when I hear the worst news in the world, it is from Mrs Sour that I hear it. It is undoubtedly good that I hear it when I'm at home, in my own kitchen, near to my own dear friends.

The old woman announces it loudly to me, me to whom she hardly ever speaks. She just stands there in the kitchen and says it. At first I don't understand. Who is this Cumberland that she speaks of? Then I remember. He is the king's son. He is the leader of the king's armies, the Red Coats.

"There will be celebrations up and down this land, and all throughout the colonies," says Mrs Sour. "Great Cumberland parties are to be held, with wonderful foods, not this peasant muck you're feeding my son."

I stay quiet, waiting for the rest, still for a moment, before the fullness of this tale is told.

"He defeated the Jacobites on Culloden Moor, near Inverness," she says, like she's savouring every word. "Completely crushed them. In less than one hour. What a hero of men."

"Completely crushed them?" I say the words; I hear the words, but I can't take them in. They don't sound real.

"Oh, they say some have escaped," she says. "But they'll be rounded up in due course and hung, drawn and quartered, as they should be."

"What's this?" says Michael, coming into the room, looking from me to Mrs Sour.

So she tells him. "The Scottish Jacobite rebellion is quashed, every last one of them killed."

I don't want to hear this. It's sour and foul. I walk back to the fire. And the broth pot.

Mrs Sour speaks some more. "And Scotland is to be dealt with firmly."

I stir the pot, rich with Scottish goodness. Wee turnips. And barley. Michael ordered that. Pot barley. Good for the belly. Good for the soul. To be served with bannocks and butter and cheese.

"The Highlanders are to be starved and thrown out of their houses. And castles." There is such glee in the sour voice, such false righteousness, like a sharpened long sword swinging, slashing through tartan and flesh and bone.

The big wooden spoon falls from my hand. I watch it and it seems to take a long time to land, it just falls and falls, a wee splash of broth here, another there, and then it lands and bounces across the wooden floor of the kitchen.

I'm not a broth spoon. I don't bounce when I fall.

Chapter Thirty-seven

It's all cold and wintery in the stone circle. Which is strange because it's summer in Pennsylvania, Penn's Forest as that name means. The old oak forest that surrounds the castle is heavy with snow, and the tall stones of the circle are topped with a small pile of white each. I walk the circle, knee deep in the densely packed snow. I feel the strain on my thighs as I push through it. There's more to come too; the sky is that special dark grey colour, almost black in places as it carries more winter our way.

Then I see her. And I recognise her. It's the Mermaid grandmother! She's standing on the fallen stone in the circle, and she's smiling at me. She holds out her hands and I trudge towards her, happy to see family in this dream I'm having. Aye, I'm nae stupid; I ken it's a dream.

She's shorter than me, the Mermaid, much shorter. She puts her hands on my face and I see that she's crying, crying for me. I want to tell her: no, I'm all right. There's no need to worry about me. Then she puts her hands flat on my chest and it warms as if my heart is glowing. And I realise that it's me that's crying.

I'm clinging onto someone in the dark, sobbing and sobbing and I know I'll never stop. I canna bear it. I canna bear that he would have suffered. My father. He would have been hurt and in pain. He would have been treated rough and known many cruelties. What if he's nae even released into death yet? What if he's in some prison, some place that smells of filth like the ship? Torture. There might be torture. It's too much. I canna take it.

Everything's black for a long while. A most affa long while. And that's good. I canna be in the light right now. Someone makes me drink something. I dinna like it. I fight them off and crawl back into my cave.

And who do ye think is in there? The Bear of course. My many-greated grandfather. He's a right big manny. But nae coarse in any way. Nae rough or cruel. I dinna like what he says though. The Mermaid didna speak. I liked her better.

"Sometimes you just have to be brave and go on," he says. "You need to open your eyes and look at the people around you, the ones who still live. Hiding away is niver the way. Wake up and be your bigger self, Granddaughter."

The utter cheek! Be your bigger self? Easy for someone of his size to say. I ken I'm tall but… I also ken he's right, and I don't much like it. I want to stay asleep and dreaming. So it's some time before I take his advice. And then it's really just something that happens. I open my eyes and find myself looking directly at Michael. He is asleep in a chair beside my bed. Wait a minty! Beside his own bed, in his own room. The cheek! Why am I here? I make to get up, all in a rage like, but I canna. There's no strength in my arms and legs. My head whirls and sparks when I lift it from the pillow, so I lie back down. And for a bit I don't think on any of it. Any of the reasons I might be here. I just look at Michael.

He looks so young when he's sleeping. His golden hair is messed, but it still makes a beautiful contrast to his sun blessed skin. He's so handsome. So fair. My thoughts are strange. Confused. Thoughts I shouldn't think.

So I just look at Michael and try not to think. I really don't want the thinking to start. Michael has a kind face, a perfect face really. I've never known anyone look quite the way Michael looks. So tall and strong and beautiful. But I don't think he thinks of himself like that. And that's sad.

His eyes are open, dark and bleary for a moment before he focuses on me and smiles. And that's a bonny sight! I smile back, though I don't attempt to lift my head from the pillow again.

"Beth?" he says, like he's not sure it's me.

"Aye."

"How are you feeling?" he asks, standing up. "Can I get you something? A drink? Chocolate? Porridge? Broth?"

I wonder who's been making those things while I've been in bed. Because I ken I've been here a while. A good few minties. But I shake my head. "Not yet. I don't want to remember it all yet." If I keep looking at Michael and nothing else, then maybe I won't. I can stay in some sort of strange dreamy land where nothing bad has ever happened.

He sits back down, and I notice how tired he looks. "I've been reading you stories," he says, holding up a book. "Mr Franklin sent some books from his library."

"What's the book?"

"Don Quixote."

"Read on."

So he does. And it really is a marvel of nonsense. But it's nice listening to Michael's voice. Comforting.

"Don Quixote is a complete fool," I decide.

"He is."

"But Michael, I'm most affa hungry." It can't be ignored any longer.

Michael calls for the others, and I cry a bit when I see them: Comfort and Nivvie and Bear.

"The quine's awakened!" declares Comfort, clapping his hands together.

They immediately fetch all the foods. All the food. And chocolate. It makes me dizzy. Bread and cheese seem to be all I can take. I understand better how Michael and Comfort came to eat mainly this when they stayed up here. It's such simple food. Easy to eat, and fortifying.

Michael stays. He always stays. Every day. He reads more books to me. One is a history book of America.

"Columbus was a fool too," I say. "Who could confuse this land for India? And then continue to call the people Injuns even once you ken you're wrong."

"You're feeling better, Beth," he says.

It's true. I've sat up, right up, and I do not feel dizzy. I also feel much less weak.

Michael goes.

Nivvie helps me to get dressed.

And then: I have to remember.

Chapter Thirty-eight

I spend a lot of time sitting outside on the porch. Michael and Comfort move an old table out there and I eat my meals and talk to people and play with Lil Thomas all in that one place.

I don't cry. Not much. Hardly ever. I think I cried a lot when I was ill. When I was 'nae weel' as we say back home. Home. Scotland. Sometimes I feel them so strong in the night, the terrible thoughts and imaginings of all that has happened there in my own country, that I canna sleep, and I go and stand in the kitchen where Michael oftentimes appears and holds me until I am sleepy, and then I return to my own wee bed in the downstairs room. We don't speak during those night-time hugs. And we don't speak of them during the day.

I wonder if Peter has heard the news of what transpired on Culloden Moor? I try to remember if we ever discussed the uprising, and I absolutely cannot recall if we did or not, which is disturbing. I also realise I canna properly bring to mind Peter's face. Maggie I have clear. But Peter is like some basic boy face on a man, or man face on a boy, all mixed up like, and it distresses me something sare. Why has this happened? Maybe it's all the upset, the grief I've been through that's done it. Aye, that must be it. It'll come right as I get better, and get better I must.

I start to make food again, to stand and stir, and help Nivvie a bit, and I'm just beginning to almost feel some sort of satisfaction from it when everything changes again.

Mrs Sour dies. Quietly like. Probably the best way for anyone to go. Just in her sleep.

Michael disna cry. He shrugs. And sighs. He doesn't say it, but there's relief in him. He's free now in a way that he's never been before.

But Sarah, poor Sarah, is beside herself with grief. She sobs and tears at her clothes in the church at the funeral. We try to take her home with us, but she won't have it. She's staying in Mrs Sour's house and no one can change her mind. Comfort and Nivvie and Lil Thomas move in with her. For now. Michael and I can manage alone for a bit.

We make chocolate, just the two of us, back in our house. "That must have seemed real strange to you, Beth," says Michael, as we sit down outside with our cups. "Sarah, I mean."

"Aye," I admit. "Mrs Sour was none too nice to her from what I saw. I guess there was more to their relationship."

"Oh, there was. Are you ready for a story?"

I am. I look at him expectantly.

"It was a secret until I was born," he starts, then pausing. "You see, it looked like... well..."

"Like what?"

He looks away, awkward. "Her baby was not white, Beth."

"Whose baby?"

He looks back at me. "My mother's. Mrs Sauer. Me. I am not a white man."

And I look at him. Oh. I see it now. He is paler than any black man I have ever seen. But he is not white. "I didn't realise that," I say. Don Quixote and Columbus are not the only fools around.

"I know," he says. "You come from a land that is white as white—"

"Not completely."

"No, but you mainly see white folks everywhere you go, and hardly anyone else, so you're never thinking about what colour anyone is."

"In the area around the castle, aye."

"You don't assess people in the same way that most over here do. Anyway. My mother is white. She was white. And so was my father. So she was horrified when she saw me. She thought they'd given her someone else's child. And then she imagined some attack had taken place upon her person that she could not recollect. She wanted me put out of the house. So Sarah told her the truth."

I look at him. Is he going to tell me? I'm most affa intrigued noo.

"Sarah is my Grandmother. Mrs Sauer's mother."

"Fit?" That, I was not expecting. "I thought Sarah was a slave owned by the family."

"She is. Was. I'll be signing her free papers as soon as I can."

This can't be true. "But Mrs Sour treated her so badly!"

"Aye," says Michael, using the perfect inflection to make the word mean a very big yes indeed. "She never fully accepted the truth of it. Because that would have meant accepting the truth of her father taking advantage of a very young girl – Sarah – who worked in his house. When he saw the little white girl that my mother turned out to be, he claimed her as his daughter. So they moved from Virginia to Pennsylvania and told a story about his wife having died in childbirth. Mrs Sauer grew up thinking Sarah her nurse only, and then later on, just her personal slave. But she must have believed it on some level, because she kept me. My father never questioned it, never said a thing. And they didn't even tell him the truth of it, Comfort and Sarah. They didn't tell me till after we came to stay here."

"Thank you for telling me," I say, feeling quite honoured to be trusted with this family secret. "Poor Sarah." I understand what she's going through now. Really understand. I fell apart when my father died. And I ken I'm not fully put back together yet; I'm just nae letting myself think about it all too much. And Mrs Sour and Sarah, for all the cruel behaviour I witnessed, they were real close.

So we go into town to see Sarah. And Michael gives her Mrs Sour's house for her own. And a big chunk of Mrs Sour's money. And poor Sarah cries some more. But I can see that she has calmed down greatly from how she was at the funeral. She is a free woman with property now. Which I think is overwhelming for her at this moment.

Michael finds all the papers he needs and begins the process of freeing every man, woman and child on the plantation. It can't be done all at once because of laws and duties, that many times get ignored by folks anyway, but he feels we should be careful here at the plantation. We shouldn't draw too much attention to ourselves. I ken he means because of Henderson, though he disna say it out loud.

Michael also sets out his grand plan to everyone at the weekly meeting. Some of us, me included, get handed our free papers at once.

I glower down at my paper and the fake name, made up by the kidnappers, that is on it: Betty McKay.

"Maybe it's better your real name is not on record as being here," Michael says, seeing my face.

And I know that he's right. But I don't want to think about why, or about what is happening in Scotland to all those who either were Jacobites or were connected to the cause in some way. There have been reports in town. I've heard people speaking about Highlanders starved out of their homes and lands, dealt with firmly just as Mrs Sour said they would be. I long to hear from Eppy, but I also cringe away from the information her letter might contain. If she's still alive. If any of them are.

I can't think about that. So I, like so many around me, focus my attention onto Michael's grand plan for the next year.

Chapter Thirty-nine

Some folks, the ones who have been freed from slavery or released from forced indenture, we have the choice to take a wage. Or we can choose to take a share of the profits at the end of the next year's harvest. This year's profits are all to be invested in making everything bigger and better, no Mrs Sour to syphon them off now, though some will have to go on surety bonds for the freed slaves. Our share of next year's money could be more than our wage. Or it could be less. Such is the way of farming and business.

I choose the profit, because I'm getting to run another little money earner anyways which will continue to pay for my letters home. I am to extend my vegetable garden and sell the extra at market. And keep the money for myself. And, though I can't clearly think on the fact with all that's happened, should I get the chance to go home before the crop is harvested and sold, Michael volunteers the information that he will extend me an advance of the predicted profit, based on what's happening on the plantation at that time.

A tall man stands up near the back of the room. "Many of us wanted to turn the earth by our houses into gardens years ago like Miss Beth has done," he says. "Fo'man said 'twas not permitted."

Well, it is permitted now. Any who want to can create gardens and grow food, and they can keep the money if they choose to sell the produce. It seems to me that this change delights some people more than the larger business plan. The younger men are clearly excited at this chance to get their share of the profit. But some decide to have none of it; they are leaving to be nearer kin in other parts of the country. So there will be fewer of us. But we're happier. And we're free.

Rebecca is the only one to choose a wage in the end. She is happy being a cook and content with her lot, especially now she can tend a garden. She offers fruit-laden cake to two young men and they dig her land over for her. I offer them chocolate and they do the same for me. But then I go and see the digging of the plantation, the place where the larger profits will lie, and what a pure piece of nonsense I do behold. The land is being worked by men, and men alone. It is backbreaking toil, and so slow.

I go home to Michael, who is busy making up orders of all the things needed. "You need to add extra horses and a plough," I tell him. "You'll get far more land covered, far more quickly that way."

"Yes, yes!" he says, excited. "We could extend out to the east as well. The plantation covers a much larger area than is currently being worked. We have to remember though, Beth, the more we plant, the more has to be maintained and harvested. And we have fewer workers now. I'm going to have to get out there and lend a hand myself."

And he does. And it is wonderful to see. Michael comes home tired and sweaty and hardly leaning on that stick at all now. Each day, it's like watching him become more of who he really is. His hair lightens under the sun and his skin darkens. That happens to most folks of course, but in Michael the contrast was already great and beautiful. Now his beauty has reached ridiculous levels.

Mine has not. The sun makes my skin red and peely. I have to stay hidden under a wide brimmed bonnet, but I still redden and blush in the strong August sunshine.

I go to see the new plough being worked and it is, indeed, hugely increasing the speed by which more land can be turned to profit. But for the first time since the grand plan was put in motion, I sense that not everybody is completely happy with the situation. Bear growls as one of the indentured servants walks past.

"Just try it, laddie," says the man, Scottish like me. He was speaking to Bear. And it was not friendly. He looks at me. "Friend to animals and just onybody, aren't ye?"

"Only good animals and onybodies," I say.

"So what goes on in that house?" he sneers. "At night, like? What's the sleeping arrangements?"

Bear takes a step towards him, growl louder now, and the man backs off, laughing. And I don't like it. I don't like any of it. Oh, I ken folks will gossip about most anything rather than look at themsels, but this feels like more than that somehow.

I look at the workers in the field and they are partly divided up: black and white, in their groups together. There are some standing together, with anyone, not caring. And for the first time I'm aware that those that mind about this sort of thing dinna like those of us that dinna mind. And that trouble could come from it. I'm not sure if I should say anything to Michael, who has a foot in both camps of folks. But of course, he already kens. It's me that's been slow to understand all this about the colour of folks' skin. Not that I'm quite there yet. I mean, for why should it matter? What a load of nonsense it is.

Michael has made us all the same here, or that's what he's trying to do. I suppose we're not all quite the same. Him and I live in the best house. The cook house is better than the field workers'. The indentured servants, having sold their indentures in the legal and proper way, have not been freed as they were not slaves, and are working out their time here as originally agreed. Maybe they feel hard done by? Their lot has not improved any, while that of others has.

Maybe that's all it is. A little bit o' jealousy. And that's everywhere between people.

I see Michael busy explaining something to some of the indentured servants, pointing over at the forest, and I walk out to them, keen to hear what is being said. He's detailing exactly where the boundaries of the land to be ploughed lie. Some bits are to be left. The woodland owned by the plantation is to stay as woodland. And that's good. It's real bonny in there. I walk home that way, between the trees and the misty looking sunbeams that are shining down through the branches to the earth. Bear runs ahead and I feel a bit sad that we're not headed into the woods to meet the quines, like in the past. But it's good that we're all happy and safe in this beautiful world.

And then I see something I've never seen before in my life. At first I think it's fairies flying up out of the tobacco as we walk past, and I do stand and stare with my mouth open a minty! But no, they're wee bugs. Wee bugs all lit up with bright shiny light. Fireflies! That's what they must be. They're golden. The sky beyond is a dark blue-grey and it's the most amazing sight I've ever seen. To think, I used to dream about exotic things such as this, and here I am, right in the midst of them. Elizabeth Manteith of the castle is standing here in America, watching fireflies fly up into the sky.

I stay there so long watching the wee golden lights that Michael is already abed when I return to the house, else I might have made him run back out there with me to see them. I would, at least, have told him about the fiery wee sprites so his dreams could have been filled with them too.

Chapter Forty

My body kens this time. My heart's beating fast, and my breath is as quick as the fireflies I've just been dreaming of, but sleepy thoughts fade fast from my mind as I focus on the noise that wakened me. It's nothing good that's here, that's happening noo; there's some trauma to come, some drama to be experienced. That's what loud banging on the house door in the middle of the night always means, and yet, and yet… we always deal with it. We always come through. That's what I'm telling myself as I approach the door. And it's the comforting thought I'm still thinking as I turn the key, hearing Michael moving about upstairs.

The thought falters a little as I look upon the sheriff and his men, and I rather wish Comfort were here too, but he is still at Sarah's house in town. "Is this the house of Michael Sauer?" says someone, maybe the sheriff, maybe one of the men. My wits are scattered. My body was right in its first reaction, and the soothing thoughts that came after were wrong. This is something terrible. This will not be so easy to come through. I ken it in my bones and in my hand that shakes as I hold the door open to them.

In they come as Michael arrives downstairs. And they're asking all sorts of questions now they ken that this is Michael Sauer himself in front of them. Henderson. It's about him. The Fo'man. Him, who we thought was dead and gone from this place forever. Him, who we never mention. He's risen up to haunt us now. I mustn't say that though. I ken that. Through all the questions and Michael's answers and Michael's eyes looking deep into my eyes every so often, I stay quiet. I listen. I nod. And then I say: "That's right. I mind on that."

It's a lie. Michael has told it and I have backed it up. He's telling them about the time Henderson came here with Mrs Sour, the time he left his dog behind. He's saying that's the last time we saw or heard of the previous foreman of the plantation.

"Why was he dismissed?" asks the sheriff.

"For violence and cruelty against the workers," Michael tells him.

"Against the slaves you've recently freed?"

"Some of them, yes," says Michael.

The sheriff's lip raises at one side in a sneer at that. Well, I canna have that.

"Oh, it's true," I tell them. "The day after I came here, Henderson had a pregnant woman tied to a post, and he was whipping her something fierce. He dragged me out to that post too, by my hair."

The sheriff looks at me, straight at me, but not deep into my eyes. "Women, dogs and slaves; they have to be disciplined. Is that the dog?"

"Yes," says Michael, his eyes begging me to be quiet, not to rile up these mannies.

"He's a good dog," I say, plenty riled up myself, but trying to hide it.

"We've had reports that Mr Henderson came back here to get him and that a shotgun was fired. And he's not been seen again since."

"We know nothing about this," says Michael, real quick before I can speak.

"And then today," says the sheriff. "A body's been found. And I suppose you know nothing about that either?"

We don't. We really don't.

"Where was it found?" says Michael, genuinely perplexed now. Or perhaps just genuinely worried. Real worried.

"In a bit of woodland," answers the sheriff, "The bit you're turning over to tobacco."

That's not right. The woodland was not supposed to be touched. Who has done that? Who has done this? I think I ken. I bet I ken. That mean faced Scotsman who spoke so crudely to me the other day. Him and his cronies. Them that thinks they're better than the rest of us, for not being slaves, women or dogs I suppose. For being white, aye I ken it; it's them.

The sheriff and his men are taking Michael with them, to see the place and the body.

"Stay here," says Michael to me. "Keep Bear with you."

And off they go. Well! What am I supposed to do? I'm trying to think so hard I canna think. Which is stupid. But oh! What do those ill-natured white mannies know? What do they actually know? Not everyone was around that night when Henderson died. I don't think many of the indentured servants were there. Not the mean ones anyway. If they were, they'd know, they'd have said it was me fired the gun and that Bear did the deed. So they don't know. But what are they at? What are they after?

I wait and I wait, and I wait some more. It's unbearable, so I take Bear down to the village, lantern in hand. I go to see Rebecca; I wake her; she knew nothing of this, of what is taking place in the woods, or of what was found in the woods. We wait together.

Wait. Wait. Wait.

The more time passes, the more unbearable it becomes. The first light of dawn can be seen in the sky now and I run back to the house with Bear. No Michael. I run to the woods with Bear. I don't know where to look – the woods are large – but there's no sound of voices and no Michael.

Village: no Michael.

House: no Michael.

Fields, now the sun is up and the day has properly begun: the indentured. I walk straight up to them and glare at them in question.

"They've teen 'im," says the Scot, a man I am not proud to name as my countryman; he smiles as he tells me this. He shows his very horrible teeth to me, like a snarling dog.

I don't let myself shout or hit out at this man, though I want to. "Teen him where?" I ask.

"The gaol," he says and I turn and run.

Chapter Forty-one

I run to Rebecca again.

"I have to tell them Bear did it," I say to her, tears leaking out of my eyes as I speak. "They have Michael, and they may kill him for it. If they think he murdered the Fo'man, that's right, isn't it? That's what'll happen? So I have to go say Bear did it after I told him to. I said 'Get him, Bear,' and it's my fault. I have to tell them."

"Calm down, girl," says Rebecca, ushering me towards the bench in the cookhouse. "What we all did that night was done to save Nivvie, and Lil Thomas. We know what could have happened to them if that man hadn't been stopped. But, you tell me the whole thing you're planning to say to these law mannies."

I tell her. But I canna calm doon. And I canna sit doon. I have to take the horse and go to the gaol.

"You can't do that," she says. "You can't tell that tale, for then they will question why you didn't say it before? And why didn't Michael? It'll look made up to cover up a planned killing."

Bear licks my hand, unaware that his future is hanging in the balance. "I will go to Comfort and Sarah first," I decide. "They might know what to do. If Michael has a law man to help him at least."

It's a plan. It's something to hold onto. I run home and make myself swallow some bread and cheese and a wee sup of ale that's sitting on the side. I shut Bear in the house, unable to look at him properly, unable to think about him, my mind is that set on Michael, as it has to be.

I walk round the side to fetch the horse, my trusty mare that takes us to town whenever we want, my sturdy mare that helped me to search for Peter, and who will now take me to help Michael. The men who dug my garden built her a wee stable up here by the house on the day that she came home from market. She replaced the older horse, Michael saying she would be better for me to ride while off out looking for Peter. It felt as if she was the horse I should have got that day in Aberdeen, that fateful day of the kidnapping, and the sailing, and the day that brought me to my true love.

And here she is, looking out at me, but she's feart. It's obvious. She disna want to come out, as if she knows that bad things are afoot.

"We have to be brave, quine," I tell her. "We have to go and find a way to help Michael."

But she cowers back in her stall, blowing fright out her nostrils, and then I hear the thing that is really scaring her. It's like a speaking growl from behind me, a loud 'grumph' sound.

So here I am again, face to face with a bear. It's the same bear I met when I was brand new to this land. I see the wee nick missing from its lug, and there he goes again, standing up and roaring.

"I hinna got time for this," I tell the creature, who then stands down onto all fours and listens to me. "I've got to go and get Michael, or at least do something about him. So, let's wish each other well and go our own separate ways."

The bear looks at me. The bear walks nearer. So near I can hear its breath. Oh damn. After all this, to be eaten by a bear, in a land so far from home.

"My great, great, great grandfather was a bear," I tell it proudly, refusing to show any fear. "In Scotland, where I come from."

The bear sniffs the air around me, as if checking the truth of this. It raises its head and 'grumphs' again, then turns and wanders away through my vegetable garden and disappears into the forest beyond. So, again, it did not eat me. I decide to take this as a good omen; well, it canna be a bad one anyway. And maybe I need to be more like the bear, nae crying as I tell my tale. Tall and roaring and brave. Aye, that's what I'll be. A big brave grandchild of a bear.

Two minutes later I find myself crying again, greeting like a wee bairn that's lost its mummy. Which I suppose I did, a long time ago. But that's nae fit's making me greet. It's the saddle. I seem to have lost the ability to do up the straps and fasten it properly. My hands are slippy with tears like a babe… as if I had been really frightened by the bear after all.

A babe and a bear.

A bear and a babe.

And suddenly I ken exactly fit to de, and, saddle straps dealt with quickly, I set off at a fair speed for Philadelphia.

Comfort and Sarah are greatly distressed by the news of the night's events. They really do seem like frail little old people in this moment, and their worry about Michael is hampering their ability to help. I also feel shaky and much less sure of my plan now that I'm speaking it out loud to them and, most importantly, to Nivvie as she was the one who was attacked that night.

Happily, Nivvie is fully supportive of the idea. "Yours was one of the very few white faces round us that night," she says. "The others didn't come to see what Fo'man was at; they weren't bothered about what was being done to me, so they don't know a thing about what went on!"

Once we are all fortified with tea, Comfort goes to see Michael's law man – thank goodness he does have one – and I go to find Mr Lay, because I think he can help, which means riding into the forest again. I do so want to rush to the gaol, but I could make it all worse if I go barging in there, saying the wrong words.

Thankfully, Mr Lay is at his house, his cave house, in the woods, and, after hearing the story of the night and the day that has just happened, he does think my plan will work and he knows other men, other white mannies who the law men may listen to, who can help us more.

By the time I make it back to Comfort and Sarah, the lawyer is there, and I tell him the plan.

"So it's true, is it?" he says. "About the bear?"

Ah. "Aye, bears has been seen around the plantation," I say. "I was aggressed by one just this morning as I set out to come here. A huge one. Quite capable of killing a man. The possibility could surely be looked into?" That's all true anyway. And it's what he has to tell the judge.

And then – I am so glad – Sarah gives me some bread and cheese and cake and ale, all in a basket, for me to take to the gaol.

Chapter Forty-two

At first I don't think they're going to let me in, the two mannies I meet when I enter the stone prison on the High Street. But a gift of cake has them allow me through to the back, and I finally get to go and see Michael.

I see Michael. And I so wish I were not seeing him thus. First I see the dirt, and my mind wonders how he came to be so dirtied in so short a time in prison. He is worse than when I came off the boat even. But then I see more. I really see. And I see him wishing that I wisna seeing.

He's been beaten. He's all cut and bruised and bloody.

He comes forward and takes my hands through the bars. I hold on tightly. I will not cry. That will only make things worse for him. So I lean my forehead in, and he meets me with his, and I whisper all about the bear to him, and tell him the law manny will be here to see him soon and everything is going to be all right. I feel strange saying that last bit, because how can I really know that? Could I not be telling Michael a lie that won't help him in the long run? But no, it feels right to say it, and it feels like it's true anyway.

"You must eat," I say, pulling away from him, not wanting him to see that I am near crying. "I've got lots of things for you." I bend down to pick up the basket which must have fallen when I seen him first.

"I'm not hungry Beth," he says, dark eyes never leaving mine.

"But you must eat. You will eat." Bossy is good. Bossy is strong. I hold onto this fact now, instead of Michael's hands: a person must eat.

My perseverance works. Michael eats. Some bread. Some cheese. And some cake. Then I push ale on him, cup through bars, and he drinks that down too.

"Time for you to be off." It's not Michael that says that. At first I think it is, and it's odd and confusing and wrong in the dingy gaol room. But it's one of the guard mannies speaking from behind me. He reminds me of the guard mannies on the boat. Bad men all.

I want to say something cutting and haughty to the man, something that will let me stay longer, something that will keep Michael safe. But I have to be careful. I ken that. My temper could make it all worse.

"I will come back tomorrow," I say to the manny, but really it's Michael I'm telling. "With fresh baked cake again."

And I do.

And the day after that.

And after that. On and on it goes.

Michael gets thinner. But he always smiles when he sees me.

Sometimes there's other men in there with him. Sometimes there's not. They all come and go faster than Michael. Why is it taking so long for him?

I demand this of the law man when I see him at Comfort and Sarah's house.

"This isn't long," he says, and he looks at me all dismissive like, as if I'm stupid.

I dinna much like the law manny. And I'm nae convinced he's doing his best to get Michael freed at all. It's all got to go to court. And that takes time.

Well, it's time wasted if you ask me. Michael should be back at home with me, eating good meals, and working the plantation to get it all ready for next year's big profit making venture.

Not that I'm actually at home. I'm staying at Sarah and Comfort's house, so as to be nearer the gaol. Sarah shows me up to my room which used to be Michael's room when he was a boy, but it feels sad in there and I canna sleep. Michael wisna happy here, and he's not happy where he is. He needs to be at home.

I ride home, back to the plantation house, and what do I discover there? Thievery and treachery! The house is in turmoil, having been raided and burgled. Oh, I ken who's done it too. It'll have been those rotten, nasty, white indentured servants that have gone and robbed

Michael. I don't know how much they took, but they've fairly messed the place up. The money box is gone. I'm not sure what else.

I set to and tidy up. It's all I can do. I stay up all night doing it. Cleaning away the filthy handprints of bad men. Putting to rights the rooms, putting everything back in its proper place. Polishing. Sweeping. Gathering the broken objects, glasses and plates mostly. A chair is ruined too, all in pieces. The rogues!

I've got Michael's room all perfect for when he comes home and it feels like a relief. I must fetch Bear from Rebecca soon. I must wash the kitchen floor too, for though it's tidy now, it still has the feel of a place that's been invaded by enemies. But it's nice up here. It's cosy too. The sun during the day must have warmed it, the heat rising up from the rest of the house as well. Michael's bed is all freshly made for him, and so comfy, so perfect, so warm.

I can hear a wee bird twittering outside the window. And the sound of an owl. I wonder if it's that tiny wee owl I saw when I was first in this land, running away into the forest. I can hear a bear too. That bear. My bear. Or I think I can. I've become so lovely and relaxed and floppy and cosy here you see… it's hard to tell what's a dream and what's real.

Chapter Forty-three

I've only gone and slept all night in Michael's bed! Or, on it, to be more precise. I'm still holding the cloth I was using for cleaning. My fingers are all pruny with absorbed dampness. And what time of day is it? I have to get to the gaol.

I get up so fast I feel dizzy. I run down the stairs so fast that I fall down the last few. I pick myself up and run into the kitchen. It's all right. It's early. I have time to make cake. And light the oven. No. Broth! That's what he needs. I set it all going and then run as fast as I can down to the cook house. I need bread and cheese to go with it all.

Bear jumps all over and up on me. It is so good to see him. And Rebecca. And Nivvie, recently returned from Sarah's house.

I tell them everything that's been happening in town.

And they tell me everything that's been happening here. About how they all decided it was right to keep working as hard as possible on the plantation, that that was the best they could do for Michael, and how the indentured servants, some of them anyway, didna like it. 'Why should we help a mulato?' they'd said, and off they'd gone, stopping by the house that they knew was empty on their way, no doubt.

The rotten men had shouted and raged down here in the village before they left. All about how a place run by nigras was never going to be any sort of success and they was leaving. Well good! I hope they've gone far away! They probably have, seeing as they took money and maybe many other things too – I dinna ken all that was took – and could end up in the gaol themselves for it.

I decide that I'm not going to tell Michael about the robbing. Not just now, anyway. He has enough to contend with, without worrying about that. But I take him chocolate today. It's not hot by the time I get to the prison of course, and some of it has spilt on my dress, but he's happy to have it. The guard mannies get none of it. Dry cake for them only. I'll have to be careful though, best make them something better tomorrow.

I tell Michael the good news, about how everyone is working so hard at home to get the extra land cleared for next year's crops, and also to harvest this year's plants, so keen are they for their profit and for him to do well too and be impressed when he comes home. I speak as if there is no doubt that he will be there at the house and plantation again soon. What am I thinking? Of course he'll be there, I canna let thoughts like that creep in.

But they do. In the middle of the night mostly. I start off in my own box bed. I always doze off at first and sleep for a bit. But then I wake up and think. And I wander all about the house. And I always end up sleeping the last bit in Michael's bed. Eppy used to say people who live by themselves can go a bit strange with no other body there to check them. I wonder what she would say if she could see me now? I wonder how her and Jock are faring? But I canna think about that either, else it all gathers round me in the darkness and I feel crushed by the weight of dreadfulness.

Days.

Weeks.

Months.

Winter's just about on us now. There's no fireflies to rise up out of the crop against dark skies anymore but there would have been no joy in it anyway, no beauty. It's just another day of cake, bread, cheese, chocolate, gaol, Comfort and Sarah's house, and then back here.

Off I set. And then, I'm faced with a scene from my worst night time imaginings.

I ken something's nae right at the door of the gaol. The guards take their cake, but there's laughter in their eyes, and it's not friendly. It's mean. I go through to the jail room and there's Michael lying on the floor with his back to me.

"Michael!"

He disna move.

"Michael!"

He grunts.

I run back through to the mannies. "Ye need to open the door and let me in. Michael's nae weel."

"Nae weel, is he?" replies the man, maybe not understanding my words, I dinna ken. "Will we let her in, then?"

Aye. They agree. They let me in.

I rush over the floor of stone, straw all about like it's a place for animals. I kneel beside Michael and put my hand on his shoulder. He turns and looks at me and roars. It's not him! It's a fierce old mannie who laughs and shouts up into my face, covering me in foul spittle.

"Where is he?" I ask the guards, marching out of the prison room. "Where is Michael?"

"How should we know?" one of them says, and that's all I get from them.

My wee horse and I have never travelled so fast. Dust rises all about us as we gallop past red brick buildings to Sarah and Comfort's house. I don't even knock like I usually do; I just barge right in. And there's Michael sitting in the parlour, all clean and in new clothes, being served tea by Sarah's new maid, the one she hired so Nivvie could go back to the plantation.

I just stand there and stare. Am I dreaming? How can this be?

"Beth," he says, standing, taking a step towards me.

I take a step away.

"They had a doctor examine the body, you see," says Comfort at my side. "There was teeth marks of an animal with sharp teeth in his neck bones. So they knows the Fo'man was not killed by a man. And it could have been a bear."

"So it's over?" I ask. "You're free, Michael?"

It's over. He's free. I am so very very happy.

I want to jump around with joy but I canna, because I actually feel sort of limp and weak with relief. The feeling passes quite quickly. Because although Michael is safe and free, there are other truths to notice here. My dear friend is now in the home of his grandmother and uncle, which, because of how they love him, is obviously his home too. I have just been terrified and then mocked and spat on in a gaol cell because I was not considered important enough to be told of the recent changes in circumstances.

"Good day to you all," I say and march straight back out of the house. I get up on my horse and ride back to Michael's other house. His house. His home.

Where I'm the cook.

It's good I've remembered the fact.

I've clearly gone a bitty strange living here on my own. Well, enough of that!

Chapter Forty-four

I feel desperate. This is Michael's home. I need to be in mine. I need to find Peter and go home. I thought it would be easy in the beginning. Someone would know where my friend had gone. Someone would point the way. But three years have passed. No one has heard of Peter, but I could step up that search again. Aye, that's what I'll do. About home, about Scotland, I dinna really want to think. Because of all the things I dinna ken, you see.

And now that Michael's safe, now that the daily danger to him is over, I have room in my head to ponder the really big question about Scotland. Who's alive and who's not? I canna bring myself to voice the word 'dead', not even in my mind, but there you go, I've gone and done it anyway.

Even extremely short term plans are difficult, because I have no idea whether Michael is coming home here today or not, so I don't know whether to prepare food for him. But I have to eat, so I go through the steps of making broth, all the time thinking, planning. I could walk the streets of Philadelphia and ask at each and every house about Peter. I never thought to do that before. I trusted Sarah and Mrs Sour to make enquiries among the townsfolk. But just how many people did they actually know anyway? I could ride my horse out to more of the farms and plantations, travel further afield than I did before. I've allowed silly fancies and ideas of who I am in this place to form again, and it's damaged my plan. I've spent all this time baking cakes and going to the gaol every day, all the while doing nothing to find Peter. My great plan, not to mention my true love – if he is that, and does it even matter? – was neglected and I didn't even notice.

But I'm noticing something now. A distinctive sound. Horses' hooves. And the rumble of cart wheels on the track. So I pick up the broom and sweep the floor. Not that it's dirty, but it's something to do while the broth cooks. Something to take my mind off what's happening in front of the house and who's approaching.

I can see them out of the corner of my eye anyway of course. Michael and Comfort. Comfort thud thunks straight up the stairs when they enter the house, but Michael comes right in here.

"Beth," he says, and I, in my fury, spin to glare at him, in his finery.

"Would you have me prepare food for you, sir?" I ask. I do actually need to ken this; I'm nae just being angry. Nae just.

"I would have you sit and speak with me Beth."

I continue to stand there, holding my broom, but he sits at the table and I notice many things that do dent my anger. He is weakened by his time in the gaol. He's so very thin. The stiffness and pain in his leg are clearly much worse. I see the flinch, quickly hidden away, when he sits. Och, the bother of him! I put bread and cheese on the table, and apples and plums that wee Mary must have left here this morning when I was out. There's raisin cake too. It looks sweet and delicious and I want Michael to eat it. But he disna. He just speaks.

"Do you know how I felt seeing you every day in the gaol?" he asks.

I say nothing but I am irked again. Was I not even welcome there?

"I longed to see you," he says. "And I dreaded it."

The cheek! The cheek! The cheek!

He goes on. "All the time you weren't there, I waited for your light and fire to arrive, to banish the dark, but once you were there I couldn't bear that you were seeing me that way."

Aye, well, I did ken that last bit, and I sit down at the table beside him.

"I wanted to be clean to see you. To look well and fed, a free and capable man. Comfort was to go and meet you at the gaol this morning, but he left it too late."

"Well it made me feel that I was as nothing to you!" I say, banging my hand on the table, everything suddenly bursting out of me in a passion. "Just some servant who didn't even warrant telling you were free. I am so very glad you are, but I'm really angry!"

"And I love you for it," he says, smiling his real smile, not the ghost of it that I've seen these past months. He fair lights up when he smiles, does Michael, almost as if there's two of him: smiling Michael and not smiling Michael.

I push the raisin cake towards smiling Michael.

Still he doesn't eat. He smiles and he speaks. "You are my dearest dear," he says. "My dearest friend."

And he is mine. It is the truth. It is why I was so angry. I reach out my hand and take his and we sit there like that for a bit. Like smiling idiots. His hand is much larger than mine. Mine looks so pink and white and delicate being held by Michael's big strong hand. I feel the beauty of the world return a little as we sit together in the kitchen.

I tell Michael about the fireflies. I tell him how they rose up out of the tobacco at dusk at the end of summer, and how it looked like magic, their little lights against the dark blue-green of the sky and forest behind. I don't tell him of my relief after he went into gaol, that there were no fireflies to watch. I would have felt nothing in seeing them then, and I don't want to make him feel sad again. I know that I could look at the fireflies now, if they were still in season, and truly admire and take delight in them once more. Michael tells me that the fireflies are a good sign, a sign of healthy soil and abundant crops.

Then I tell Michael of my darkest thoughts, the ones I canna even face myself most of the time. How it was my fault that the Fo'man got killed. How it wasn't the first time either. How I pushed First Mate Alexander Young, and how he fell through the side of the ship.

"But, Beth," says Michael. "You acted against abuse. Your actions saved others. You must not continue to hold guilt in your heart for this."

I look at him, wishing I could be free of the guilt, but I think it's one of those things that is easier to say than it is to feel.

"I understand though," he says. "For a long time I believed I killed my father."

"But that was an accident, Michael! And you were just a child."

"As were you," he says. "But I know. Now, I know."

I squeeze his hand and feel a lightening of my own guilt too. And then we're silent there at the table again. It's a perfect quiet moment between us. Between other moments. And then I hear it. And so does he. The other moment coming. Feet running towards the back door. Hands hammering on it, excited and full of news.

I open the door to everybody: Rebecca, Mary, Nivvie, Samson, Lil Thomas.

They are delighted to see Michael, and so relieved that he is home and safe and well.

I wait. For this is not why they came. They did not know Michael was here, did not know he was free even. Rebecca tells Nivvie to put the pot on for tea as she takes papers out of her apron. Two letters. Both for me. They arrived on the same ship, so Rebecca says. One is from Eppy. I ken the writing on that one. The other is in some unknown hand. Somehow I know it's a male hand. An authoritative hand. The hand of a fine gentleman, perhaps?

I turn this second letter over and see the seal. It's one of the Manteith seals, the one with the crest, the one Eppy used before but that she is not using now. There's the Mermaid. There's the Bear. I remember the metal seal that made it. I remember sitting on my father's lap and turning the seal on its stiff wee hinge to see all three choices that a letter writer had at their disposal. There was this one and then one with secret Jacobite symbols and then one with arms. I printed them all into wax that day with my father, but I always liked this one the best.

After this, I dinna think I will.

Chapter Forty-five

It's too scary, the letter from the unknown writer, someone who has my father's seals but is not my father, so I put it aside and read Eppy's with everyone sitting round. I read it out loud so I am not alone in the hearing of what I ken is going to be bad news.

Dearest Miss Elsie,

I hope that you are still doing well in your American house, dearie. Things are not so well here. I dinna ken if you will have heard what took place on Culloden Moor this April but things did not go well for the Jacobite lads.

But yon Laird fae the castle survived. He is captured and awaiting the decisions of the king, but he is alive. I thought you would like to ken this, being as how you came from aroon about here.

Jock and me have moved into the cottage the other side of the pool, as the castle has been taken by the Red Coats. But dinna you worry about us. We have plenty oats and onions to keep us going right into next year!

I will write again when there is more to tell you, and I hope you will write to me at the cottage here.

You keep yersel warm and cosy in that big country, my quine!

Eppy

"She's saying your father's survived," says Comfort, having come down the stairs at some point. "That's a good thing, Miss Beth."

I nod. It was a good thing when Eppy wrote this letter. But it's no longer true. In the months that have passed, my father will have been treated as any other traitor to the crown. He is not of this earth now. I ken the truth of it right through my body, but I've nae let it right into my heart yet. I feel hollow like an old bone that a dog has gnawed all the goodness from as I open the second letter, and Michael moves his chair round the table to sit right beside me.

The second letter does not absolutely confirm my father's death, having been written in the same month as Eppy's.

Cousin Elizabeth,

I have been told you are in the Colonies now, for why I cannot imagine, but I write to inform you that your father is being held in Carlisle and I expect him to have been executed, probably hung, drawn and quartered if the rumours are true, by the time you read this, if you read it at all.

I, a loyal king's man, have been granted ownership of the castle and all its lands. If you wish to write to me here seeking news of your treacherous parent, you may.

Your mother perished when she heard that Manteith had been taken prisoner. This may have been all the better for her as she was likely a traitor too.

Your Dear Cousin

Matthew Manteith

"I always called him nasty Cousin Matthew," I tell everyone, for they won't know who he is. "He was a cruel piece of work when he was a wee bairn, always being unkind to some creature or person."

"He still is, Beth," says Michael, his hand on my arm now. "You should try to put his words from your mind. He didn't even try to hide who you were, like Eppy did. He had no concern for your safety, using your real name like that."

"But his words are true," I say. "I ken it."

"You're an orphan like me now," says wee Mary, who really is not so wee anymore. She must count around ten years at least.

I drink my tea, black tea full of sugar, and I hold Mary's hand. And then I get ready to prepare the food. This causes great consternation among my companions. I should be sitting. Resting. Recovering from shock.

"No, I shouldn't," I tell them. "I need to go about my normal business. Michael is home, even Comfort is here for a visit. So, I'm going to cook."

It's not really my normal business though, is it, when so many bodies are keen to help me. I start to chop an onion and the knife is taken away. And I needn't even try and lift the pot onto the hook over the fire or light the oven! No, no, no. Less shaky hands than mine are doing that.

I give up. I gather my plaid about me and walk outside. Michael follows me out onto the steps and asks if he can accompany me.

"Of course. Why wouldn't you be able to come too?"

"I thought maybe you needed time to yourself? It is very busy in there." He nods back towards the kitchen.

"I'm going to see the fireflies," I tell him, and he walks with me.

Down the track we go, the forest on one side, until we come to the tobacco. "We might have to wait a wee minty," I tell him. "It's not quite dark enough for them."

So we sit on a fallen tree trunk. And we wait. And I feel fine.

"I think they like warmer times," says Michael. "You may have to wait till next year to see your fiery little friends again."

"Oh, yes." I knew that. But in this moment I didn't. My mind is working slowly, as if it only has room for particular information. I try to explain that this doesn't mean I'm really upset to Michael, but I ken he disna believe me.

"I grieved when I first knew of Culloden," I explain. They all ken that, so why all the fuss now, I don't know. "My sadness is out of me."

"Grief is a strange thing," says Michael. "You can think it's done with, and then new parts of it jump out of the dark at you and it starts all over again."

"Well it won't do that to me. My heart is strong."

He nods. Appeasing me. And then, one tiny solitary light floats up out of the crop. Having survived the cold when all the others did not. Tiny and golden, glowing and orange. With all that dark, dark blue behind. And I wait to see the beauty, to feel the glow of it like I did before. I wait, and I wait. But it disna come. It's just a bug. I'm just me. And that's that.

Chapter Forty-six

And that really is that for me for a while. I'm just here. Doing the things I do. Cooking. Though I dinna have the imagination left to do much interesting with any of it. But we eat. I dig more of my garden over for next year's produce. Michael helps with that. Stick put aside, smile on, he puts his back into the work more than me. I don't have much caring to earn a profit anymore. I have nothing to go back to. No passage to earn. No family. No castle.

The days go on. Comfort stays here sometimes, and at Sarah's house in town sometimes. I think he worries that I am not taking care of Michael properly. But I am. We always have enough to eat. It's basic. But it's better than what they were eating when I first came here.

I look for Peter though. I do that. I ride out to farms and houses all over this place of Penn's forest. I ride as far as I can go in a day sometimes and dinna get home till dark. But I dinna find him. I dinna de that.

There's one moment when I do think I have found him. A farmer mannie says they have a boy called Peter of the right age, and then he takes a most affa long time to find him while I sit in the house with the wifie, answering her questions about Aberdeen and Scotland. My heart beats a wee bit fiercer when she says, "Oh, here they come," and I stand to see. And it is not him. Even from a distance I can tell that he's a very young boy, much smaller than Peter was when I knew him. So I ride home.

And I know then it is all of no use. I ken now that I will never find Peter. If he was to be found he would have shown up long ago. So I stop trying.

Maybe he somehow made his way back home. Maybe he was taken far away by a kind employer to some well-run farm or plantation. There are dark maybes floating around in my mind too, but I keep them far away from my heart.

But there's no more search. No more notices to go in shop windows or on public boards.

That first time we had those printed up seems so long ago now. Like looking back on a different age or world. A different Elizabeth. One that still had hope.

I'm Beth now. A cook. Scottish, but sort of American too. Torn apart and made into something new. A blank page. I feel blank, anyway.

Digging in the dirt. Stirring the soup. Watching Lil Thomas play. He likes to draw pictures in the dirt. So we're both lovers of the earth and the garden.

I watch the first snow fall from the window of the kitchen. Younger, stupider, me used to think such an event exciting. Beautiful even. Now it's just dreich. The nights are long and dark, and the mornings are dull.

Michael buys me a new cloak and new boots. I look at the imprint of the boots in the snow. They have a different shape to my old ones. It's something that I ken should be pleasing but it just isna. Nothing is. I can't even remember how it really felt to be pleased about anything.

But I'm alive. And others are not. So I should be glad. I thank God for it when we go to church of a Sunday, though it feels insincere. For am I really filled with gratitude?

We go to stay in town for Christmas. Comfort insisted and we didn't resist. I ken what the old man was thinking though. He was thinking it'd be a sad affair for Michael to spend Christmas alone with me at the plantation house. Sarah will make better food. And I dare say that's right. I dare say. I don't think I used to think words like that when I lived in Scotland. But I canna remember right. It hurts to try even.

That might start the scarier thoughts that I sometimes have. Thoughts that in this state of never feeling joy I am become like a person on Laudanum. Like a walking about version of my mother. But it doesn't really matter. I don't have wee bairns to take care of.

So here we are. It's just me and Sarah that are about when I get up on Christmas morning, and she gets me all busy helping prepare a goose. And some fruit puddings. One is a dumpling, cooked in a muslin bag, like Eppy used to make. I think I'm remembering that right, but I'm nae sure.

Michael and Comfort come home from wherever they've been, and there's laughing and lots of talking and exclaiming. I don't ask what about. I didna ask why they were not here when I got up, so why would I ask about this now?

Into the kitchen Michael comes to fetch me, and his eyes are all lit up like a wee bairn at, well, Christmas. He takes my hands and leads me through to the parlour where the fire is lit and it's all warm and cosy. There's a wooden box by the hearth, and Comfort and Sarah are gazing into it in wonder. I can tell you now, whatever is in there, I will feel no wonder.

Then I hear it. The wee yip sound. It comes again. And again. And I am drawn over to the box to look in. And I canna believe it.

Prince Charles of Scotland and all the world is in there. Two of him. Just like he was when I got him. Babies. Puppies. I get down on my knees and pick one up. It squirms and wriggles in my hands but it wags its wee tail. So full of joy is it that I have picked it up. So I pick the other one up too. And hold them both to my chest.

What funny wee beasties they are, licking and licking at my face.

"Where did you get them?" I ask, for this is very strange. I have never seen this breed of dog here in Pennsylvania before. And they are the same. Just the same. I hold them out and away from me to make sure. They are the King Charles Spaniels with the black and the gold and the white. So small. Wee pink pads on their paws.

"We heard there was a pregnant spaniel came off a boat two months ago," says Michael. "We hoped they might be the right type for you. Are they, Beth?"

"Oh aye," I say and my voice is strange, kind of cracked in the middle. "They're just exactly the same as Prince Charles."

"Well, not exactly the same," says Comfort. "These is both girls."

Girls. Wee furry quines. I canna get enough of them. Their sweet puppy smell, and their wee tongues, and their bonny wee lugs.

And then I ken why they're so mad about licking my face. It's the salt you see. Dogs always like that. And tears is full of salt.

Chapter Forty-seven

It's fair to say that I am ruining Christmas. It starts with the puppies, them being so small and gentle and sweet like. So vulnerable. What if we hadna been good folks that would take care of them properly? What if they had been bought by nasty people like the Fo'man or the kidnapping boat mannies?

"That wouldn't have happened, Miss Beth," says Comfort on hearing my sad ideas. "These dogs were real expensive. Ruffians wouldn't be spending that sort of money on puppies."

His words slow my tears a wee bitty. Because I can hear that he thinks maybe Michael should not have spent such a lot of money on the puppies for me. And that makes me feel slightly cross at Comfort, but not enough to actually stop crying, not completely.

We sit through at the big table where the goose and all the other grand dishes that Sarah prepared are laid out. I feed my new pets wee scribblings of the goose meat and they do love it!

"Maybe you should put them down," suggests Sarah. "Have some dinner yourself."

"The dinner is wonderful, Sarah," I tell her, knowing how much work she put into it, having given the maid Christmas off like she did, but also knowing I canna eat in this moment, and that I won't be putting my puppies down. "It's all so much better than I would have made."

"I wonder how Bear will take to them," says Michael.

Bear. He's been left at home in the cook house. He'll be being spoilt, I ken. But, Bear. The very word draws me back across the sea to the land of my forbears, the Mermaid and the Bear. And all that has happened there in recent years. My father. My mother. My brother. All gone.

And here I am on foreign soil. With a rich Christmas dinner, and good people, and a good fire, and bonny new pets.

If I thought I was really crying before, now I know different. This is the real deluge, crashing and soaking like the North Sea on a stormy day against a breakwater.

My poor puppies. I carry them about the house with me as I sob, up and down the stairs, straining to breathe at times. Poor Michael. He follows. He tries to hug and hold, but I will not be hugged or held. He takes the puppies for a minty now and again, before I demand them straight back, but it gives me a moment to tear my hair and hammer my chest like a crazed woman, which I suppose I am.

By night time I ken the deepest grief. And it's not even that they are all dead. My mother and my brother: they did not suffer much. I ken that. But my father, a traitor, a Jacobite, captured and imprisoned. I canna hide fae it ony longer. He will have been tortured. I feel the vulnerability of him, the human frailty, though he was not a frail man. He will have known terrible pain and fear before he died. And it's that suffering that I canna bear.

The wee pups get used to the crying and curl up and go to sleep in the crook of my arm as I sob on and on, lying on the bed Sarah has made up for me.

Michael lies behind me. I don't have the energy to object to being held now, and besides, it feels good, like I now can't stand not to be held.

"He's at peace now," says Michael, and something in me gives.

For that is true. Of course my father is at peace. And he's in a good place. Of course. Of course. Whatever happened, it is now over. Nothing goes on forever. Truth. And then the bed feels ever so soft, and I can hear the puppies sniffly breathing right by me and feel Michael's strong and sturdy warmth behind me.

Michael's not behind me when I awaken. He must've moved. For decency I suppose. But who would ken anyway? The puppies are rolling around on the bed, playing with each other. That must have been what wakened me. And they've wet the bed. There are three distinct little wet patches on Sarah's bonny cover.

"You naughty wee imps!" I tell them, picking them up and hugging them to me.

"I'm not that bad, am I?" says Michael, still there after all, in the room, on the chair.

"They've wet the bed," I explain, and he laughs.

We sneak down the stairs and out into the windy street, unkempt and in yesterday's clothes as we are. The wee pups run about and pee again, beside a tree, where they must have smelled it was the thing to do.

"Do you want to go home, Beth?" asks Michael.

I look at him, through my madly blowing about hair, feeling strange, because: what does he mean?

"We can introduce your babies to Bear."

"Aye," I say, for I do want to do that. "I think I've spoilt Comfort and Sarah's Christmas enough," I add.

"They don't mind."

"Hmm…" I think they do, a bit anyway. How could anyone enjoy having such crazed behaviour under their roof at any time, let alone at Christmas?

So, home we go to Bear.

Chapter Forty-eight

'Tis just as well Bear is such a great soppy creature when it comes to the babies, for they test him something sare! They treat his tail as if it's a wild animal they are trying to kill, biting and pulling at it with no holds barred. He looks at me with his head tilted to one side when they do this, as if he finds it most amusing. They follow him everywhere too; he gets no peace from the pair of them at all. And then they sleep, all curled up between his furry front paws, and he licks their wee heads.

He growls when they try to eat his food though, and they do hold back then. So Bear is still top dog among dogs.

Everybody loves the furry babies. All sorts of folks come to visit from the plantation village to see them once it gets round that all are welcome to call at the house. Many, many cups of chocolate are made that winter as many, many bairns, both wee and full grown, get down on their knees to play with the puppies in front of our fire.

Winter soon deepens. Deepens in many ways. Snow is deep. My wee babies disappear into it when they run outside, Bear chasing them all over the place, feart of losing them I think. And the cold is extreme. I fill hot clay bottles for us at night to take to our beds. I canna help but think it would be warmer if we all just slept in the kitchen with the dogs and the dying fire. But it wouldna be decent. Sometimes the 'decent' ways of the world just seem a bitty daft.

I get up early and watch huge flakes of snow fall to earth. They remind me of Scotland and the castle. I light the fire, the big one in the hearth and it calls to mind the big one in the great hall of the castle. I wonder if it's quiet and still in there now, as I sit here by the hearth in America with my three doggies. It might be bustling and full of life like it used to be before Thomas died. Who knows what Cousin Matthew will have done with the place? Is he rich now? Probably. Being a loyal king's man and all. There's really no point to these wonderings of my mind, so I go and start the broth cooking.

By the time springtime comes, my babies are big, still not as big as they will be, but strong and naughty and sometimes having to be tied to stop them from digging at the newly prepared and planted earth, and held and scolded to stop them stealing whatever food is going. They take it right out of folks' hands, the cheeky wee louts. You'd think they weren't fed. And they are. Plenty well.

The farming is going plenty well too. The weather is with us, and after a month of long days of planting, we're sitting sipping cool tea on the porch. My vegetables are in. The tobacco is in. We have to watch and check for insects, and maybe late frosts, but we're doing well.

"How goes it, Beth?" asks Michael at the beginning of summer.

"I think you ken fine it goes well," I tell him as we walk alongside the beautiful fresh crop at dusk.

"I mean in your heart. How fares it?" His eyes are lit as if with the golden glow of a thousand fireflies, and for a moment I dinna ken fit he means. "It took me a long time to heal," he says.

"My father," I say, realising this is what he meant. "I still cry at night sometimes. That's when there's time to think on it. But you were right. He is at peace now."

"Aye," says Michael, and it makes me smile. I have infected everybody with Scottish words. "Harvest will be even busier this year," he says. "We have more crop to get in and dry, and less bodies to do it. Are you up to the challenge Beth?"

"I am."

He isn't wrong. Summer passes quickly and then we work from morning light until the fireflies rise, and even longer sometimes. Cutting and gathering, and carrying and hanging, and cooking extra to keep everybody going, and carrying that out to the fields. I am lucky. I get to take a turn at it all, so my back disna suffer like those who are just cutting, and my arms aren't strained like the people who carry all day.

I work my own garden too and make some coins. I keep them in a wee pot at the back of my bed. To do something with them one day. Something important. I don't think about what exactly, but: one day.

"Well?" I ask Michael as he sits at the accounts in late September.

He turns and looks at me, real serious like, in the candlelight of the upstairs room. And I think for a moment that things are not good, that there has been some financial disaster, some miscalculation, surely not more thievery? Then he smiles, his great big Michael smile, the real one, and I ken everything is all right, and I am more than a little bit vexed with him!

"You tricked me. I thought it had all been for nought."

"Ha!" he says, the complete and utter nerve of him. "We're rich men and women on this plantation tonight. Come, let's tell the others."

Chapter Forty-nine

My new boots do make a pleasing sound on the paved street as we walk along, the four of us, arm in arm. Michael and I, Sarah and Comfort. We are out on the town tonight. We wave as we catch sight of and meet others from the plantation off out to celebrate too. But Comfort says he knows the best place for us to go. It is a tavern, owned and run by a woman no less, and there will be music and dancing and much merriment late into the night. And the colour of your face does not matter.

I catch sight of us in a shop window and – oh my – we do look fine. I'm in my new blue dress, a dress with a hooped bottom, no less. It's nae quite the fashion of the ladies hereabouts – the glamorous Rachel has stopped wearing them – but when I saw it in the back of the dressmaker's shop, well, I just had to have it. My well heeled boots shine in the evening sun below the hoop. Michael is looking so handsome in his new coat, and Comfort and Sarah have dressed up too. Truth is though, they have both been quite smart and tidy and dressed up since Mrs Sour died.

'Tis quite busy in the tavern when we get there, but there's no music as yet. That is fine and well, because we are to eat first. We find a wee table in the corner, and there's roast meat and fresh bread with a different taste to that we have at home, and rich wine. By the end of the meal Sarah and I have elicited promises from both men that they will dance with us. I see Michael eye his cane and look uncertain, but I ken he will be fine. He will put his hands on my shoulders, or my waist, and we will whirl the night away. I find myself flushing a little, already a wee bit dizzied, just at the thought of the dancing.

The tavern is filling up. Michael pushes his way through the throng to get more drinks for us, Comfort going with him to help carry.

"I'm looking forward to watching you two young 'uns on the dance floor," says Sarah who is more talkative tonight than I've ever known her to be. I think it's the wine. I am feeling its warming effect myself.

"It'll be good to see you two old people waltzing too," I say, then pausing, hoping that I was not too rude, but Sarah just laughs, which is a good sound to hear. She has not done it much since the passing of Mrs Sour.

"You are just what our boy needs," she says. "I knew it the minute I saw you at the slave block. 'She'll wake him up,' I thought. I said you would be a good choice to my dear Elspeth, and that we should hire you at once before someone else got you, and she agreed. And then you did go and run off, driving us all to distraction."

"Well, I do like to do that," I say, laughing, but feeling that strange flush on my cheeks again as I think about how I came to be here, to be with these people, Sarah and Comfort and Michael.

A wee silence falls between us as I ponder what Sarah has just told me. It was her decision to buy me. And Mrs Sour—

"Mrs Sour was called Elspeth?" I ask, somewhat amazed.

"That's the name I gave her."

"It's Scottish," I say. "It's a version of my own name, Elizabeth."

"Well, isn't that a thing? I heard tell of a fine lady called Elspeth, and I took the name for my babe. And she did turn out to be a fine lady too."

It's probably just as well that before I can make any comment on the fineness of Mrs Sour, I see the men making their way back to us with the drinks. Two familiar faces in a crowd of strangers. They're both dear to me now, I realise, even grumpy old Comfort, though he's not so grumpety tonight. The wine is doing things to us all, obviously.

"It's lively through there," says Comfort, nodding to the back room where the dancing is to take place. "Think it's those Ulster Scots; they don't need music to get up a din."

Indeed, I can hear some male shouting and stamping of feet going on in that direction.

"I got you some cheese," says Michael, laying down the plate on the dark shiny wood of the table. "I know how you like it."

There's three types of cheese, and more soft white bread and pickles too!

"It's like a ploughman's meal," I say. "Back in Scotland, you give the farming men a lump of cheese, and bread and a pickle, maybe an apple too, to take with them out in the fields." I take a bit of cheese. "So good!"

"It is Beth," says Michael. "It is."

And we're smiley all round. All four of us. All happy and sweet together.

"So," says Sarah. "You've made your pretty profit. Have you thought about what you're going to do with it?"

It's me they're looking at, Comfort and Sarah. Michael is looking towards the back room again where there has been some sort of crash and dropping of plates and glasses, by the sounds of things. I'm aware of them all, Michael's turned head, and Comfort's frown as if Sarah shouldn't have asked, and her inquisitiveness, as if the question is hugely important.

"I really haven't thought about it," I say, because I haven't and I don't want to. I've made some money and that's good. I just want to have fun with my friends tonight, and go on with my life and not think about serious things. It's like there's a wee cloud round the subject of the money which I dinna understand, and I don't want there to be anything cloudy or rainy about this night.

So I eat my cheese. I persuade Michael to try a pickle. And we all drink more wine.

Then the music starts up, and I do so love the sound of it. My feet start moving at once, tap tapping on the floor. There's fiddles and pipes. It's like being in Scotland!

Michael stands and holds out his arm for me to take, such a grand lord and lady are we as we stroll through to the back with everyone else. So many bodies. Comfort and Sarah are a wee bit behind, but they're coming too.

The floor is open and clear. The musicians are set up at one end of the big room and people are just standing about round the edges, waiting for someone to be the first to dance. Their wait is over.

I face Michael and take a few steps back from him, right into the clear space of the floor, feeling many eyes on me. I perform a wee do-se-do for my dear friend whose brown eyes are smiling, and hold out my hands to him.

And then I hear a voice. A loud voice. A Scottish voice.

"I dinna believe it," says the voice from behind me, accompanied by approaching footsteps. "After all this time. It's only Lady Elizabeth of the castle!"

Everything feels slow and cloudy as I turn to look at the speaker of these words. He's tall. Not as tall as Michael, but taller than me. My hands are still stretched out. The man takes those hands and lifts them to his mouth and kisses them. And then he lifts his head back up and looks straight at me and I'm staring into the happy laughing face of Peter Williamson.

Chapter Fifty

We stand for a good few minties just staring and smiling at each other. I canna believe it! I just canna believe it! I had given up any hope of ever seeing Peter again. And he's the same. I mean, it's been the same for him since we saw each other last. We're babbling now, words and sentences overlapping as they burst out.

He looked for me. I looked for him. In all the wrong places. He looked in fine houses in Philadelphia. He knocked on a lot of doors, he says. I came closer than I thought to finding him. He kens one of the farms I name, one of those that I rode out to. He stays not far from it. Oh, the vexation!

"I wis at school for a year," says Peter. "Maybe that confused things."

"At school?"

"Aye. Wilson, the manny that bought my indentures, he let me go to school so I could learn to read and write as well as you, Elizabeth Manteith! He's an affa fine manny; he was kidnapped when he was a lad too. In Perth. So he kens fit like it is."

I'm shaking my head. It's almost too much to take in. Peter. He's an older Peter, as I am older too, but it's him. Here. Now. In the middle of this room, dancers swirling round us, music loud, and there's his voice full of the sounds of Aberdeen. I have to tell Michael!

I turn, and Michael's right there, looking as taken aback and astonished as myself. "Michael! It's Peter!"

"Yes, yes," says Michael, nodding. "You should come and sit with your friend, Beth; we should have a drink together."

I introduce the two men. "It was Michael got my indentures," I tell Peter. "He was gifted me, but he freed me and employed me as his housekeeper."

"A grand lady like yersel, cleaning hoose?"

"I'm nae so grand noo, Peter; and, truthfully, I may have just about been a Lady, but I was never really that grand."

"No, but you wis always a right fine quine, and I'm right glad to see you again."

And we're hugging. And it's a bit like being hugged by a great big bear. But in a good way. No fear of death included.

Sarah and Comfort appear, and there's more introductions and we all sit together at the side of the large room. Peter and me canna stop speaking, spikkin' as he says, and it's so good to hear someone else speak – spik – like that, and there's so much to say. We fill in the four years. Four years! The four years that have passed. We talk about Culloden. I tell him about my father. He kens folks as was mixed up in it too.

And then we get back on to talking about something I haven't thought about, not in any detail anyway, for a long time. Our journey here. Michael is shocked by some of the events. He did not know about Maggie. He did not know we were shipwrecked and left to die. He goes quite quiet. I squeeze his hand, as Peter and I speak on and on.

"Do you remember—?"

"Aye. And do you remember—?"

And then the evening is winding down. Sarah and Comfort are long gone, home to their beds. "And we never even danced!" I say, remembering the dancing plans made earlier.

"The night's not over yet," says Peter, taking my hand and standing. And to the last tune of the evening, we turn some heads and raise some American eyebrows. Scottish folk can go a bit mad with dancing, and Peter certainly does. I feel flung about all over the place to be honest. My hair's certainly all over the place and I'm breathless and sweaty by the time the music ends.

Michael invites Peter to dinner at the house on Sunday. We arrange to meet him in the centre of town after church, and travel back to the plantation together. "You can meet all my other friends too," I tell my long lost friend before we hug goodbye for the night.

"I just canna believe it," I tell Michael as we climb into the cart to ride home. "Peter! After all this time! Can you believe it? It doesn't feel real."

"He seemed pretty real to me," says Michael.

"I feel like I'll wake up and find out it wasn't true."

"Well, we'll see on Sunday if he shows up, won't we?"

I run in to the house and tell the doggies, not that they ken a bit of what or who I'm talking about, but I'm that excited. I'm humming the tune, the last one, the one that we danced to.

"Oh!" I say, seeing Michael standing in the kitchen, beside the two lanterns he's just lit, staring out into the darkness of the night. "You never danced with me, Michael. And you promised!"

"Did I?" he says, all quiet like.

"Aye," I say, holding out my arms like I did just before we met in with Peter.

"Beth," he says, as if us dancing together is something that could never happen, leaning on his cane as he is.

"Michael," I say. "Put one hand here on my shoulder and the other about my waist." And, with a little reluctance, he does, and off we go.

We're slow at first as I hum the tune, and we get the feel of the rhythm of the melody, and each other. Then we speed up a little, and a little more, until we're fair reeling about the kitchen, all happy and light and tickly feeling, the hoop of my dress swaying about beneath us. We finally stop back by the lanterns, laughing and breathless, and I gaze up into Michael's eyes. And he stares down into mine. And it's a strange moment. Like there's something big taking place. A totally happy moment though. Which is what makes what's happening now even worse.

Michael is staggering back from me, out of my arms, almost pushing me away in his effort to escape.

"Beth," he says. "Oh, Beth."

"What is it? Are you hurt?"

He doesn't answer this question. He says something else instead. "You can go home now."

"What?"

"To Scotland. The profit. I'll pay your passage, Beth. Put right the terrible wrong that was done you."

"Fit?" I'm dizzy from the dancing. I can't understand his words.

"I'll pay for Peter as well. The two of you were kidnapped together. Then lost to each other. But you can go home together now."

My heart is thumping. From the dancing. I need to be alone. I need to lie down. So I take my lantern and walk through to my bedroom and close the door and climb into bed, still in my fine new dress, the hoop of which is most affa awkward in the box bed, but I dinna care.

I dinna ken fit to think.

I dinna ken fit I feel.

And I dinna want to do either of those things. No thinking. No feeling. So I put out the lantern and stare into the darkness, keeping my mind as blank as blank can be, until sleep takes me.

Chapter Fifty-one

I move to get up at first light, and fall right onto the floor thanks to the hooped dress getting caught in the sides of the box bed, it having been a ridiculous garment to sleep in. I struggle out of the accursed thing, put on a plainer gown, and walk back through to the kitchen, to the place where Michael and I stood last night. Beside the lanterns. Beside each other. He's nae asleep. The house has that 'everyone awake' atmosphere to it that I've come to know so well, but I have no inclination to seek him out.

I feel a lot of things but the biggest one is anger. Peter turning up was such a shock, and I'm so happy for it, so happy he is safe and well... but there's confusion there too. Because Peter was meant to be my true love. I wince at the thought. It feels so childish now. And it never entered my head last night. It was a friend I saw before me, a long lost friend. But is that all he is? If we're to go back home to Scotland together... well... maybe we would grow close in that way, but that thought disna feel right at all.

And then I danced with Michael, and that was so wonderful and exciting and... well... lots of slow running wells this morning... But the wells don't matter, because dancing with me so horrified Michael that he immediately wanted to send me away. He made me feel stupid, like I shouldn't have felt I was welcome here any longer now that I can be returned to Scotland, like I should have offered to go myself. And I think maybe it was in the back of my mind, somewhere very far back, that I could do that now, that I could go. It's the cloudy thing I didna want to think about before in the tavern with Sarah and Comfort.

So. Going back to Scotland. It should be a happy thought. For sure, it is partly a happy thought. But what am I going back to? I suspect I'll be living with Eppy and Jock in their wee cottage on the other side of the pool from the castle. Deep in the woods. Almost like Mr Lay. And I'd rather that than live in any castle with Cousin Matthew. I think. Everything is confusing and upsetting this morning, and I pull on my boots to run outside with my dogs.

The air is chill, mist hanging in soft lines between the tall trees as I run in among them. I remember running into trees like this when I was first here in this land. I remember my longing to go home. It's still there. Of course it is. I sit down on a fallen tree, its bark all rough through my dress. And from the moment Peter was sold to someone different, I've wanted to find him. One want has been satisfied, the other is at hand. They happened together, and I had feared they might not. So why is my predominating emotion anger? It should be joy. I'm so angry that I'm angry at myself for being angry and it's making me cry. Enough!

I turn and march back through the woods, though not towards the house. It's Rebecca and Nivvie and Thomas and Mary that I'm seeking. I can tell them about Peter. They'll be glad for that. I dinna want to tell them the rest really, but I'd rather it's me tells it right, rather than Michael – Michael! – telling it like he's doing some great grand thing by paying to send me away.

They're all up, of course they are. They're all in the cook house, the lovely cook house. And who else is in there? Only the quines! I canna believe it. It's like a party in the wee hoosie as we hug and laugh and admire the children and dogs and each other. We've all grown and changed, even us older lassies. Wee Bethany is a proper wee quine now, dancing about with Lil Thomas as if they've never been apart. Like me and Peter were dancing about last night.

And then Eliza spoils it. She says something so stupid I canna believe it. "We both thought you'd be married to Michael by now!"

I sit down all of a sudden, my belly hurting something terrible, like it's been punched. But I have to put right this nonsensical notion. "I'm the opposite of married to Michael, thank you very much."

"So… not married to Michael?"

I'm right scunnered at Eliza now, so I just let the truth burst out real loud.

"Michael canna stand the sight of me any longer, so he's sending me back across the sea to Scotland. And Peter too. So that's the opposite!"

This brings a lot of questions. About Peter. And the sea. And Scotland. And I'm given a cup of chocolate as I try to answer them all at once. And Mary brings me a wee cake. And I try to explain one startling event at a time. Everyone's real excited about Peter, and wanting to meet him. And not really that bothered about Michael sending us away, as if they haven't taken that bit in properly.

Rebecca does say: "I wondered if that would be in your mind, Miss Beth, what with you having the money for it now."

Of course. I can pay for myself. Maybe Peter too, if we can get cheap passage. It can't be any worse than our journey here. And that thought, the paying for it myself, gives me a strange sort of pleasure. A grim pleasure. I'm looking forward to telling Michael that I need none of his money anyway.

"Will you take the doggies with you?" asks Mary.

"Oh. No," I say, at once. "They might not survive the trip. I canna do that to the wee mites. You'll have to look after them."

"Oh, I think it'll be Michael who looks after them," says Rebecca.

"Will you miss us, Beth?" asks Mary.

"Aye, I'll miss you all something fierce," I say, choking up with tears at the idea of leaving them all behind. "I'll write to you. Send you presents fae Scotland."

"I'd like a stone from the castle walls," says Mary.

"Aye," I say, thinking that that will surely annoy Cousin Matthew, and how that will be a good thing.

So they're all coming to tea at the house on Sunday afternoon now, to meet Peter, who'd better be real and show up in town after church on Sunday like he promised.

He is real. And he does show up. Which is just as well, as Michael and I have very little left to say to one another. Once you want someone gone I suppose you don't have to make polite conversation anymore. He had the cheek to appear angry at me wanting to pay for myself and Peter though. But since that, we've been most affa quiet.

So when I hear a Scots voice shouting, "There's my bonny quine!" in the street on Sunday, I am most affa relieved. Most affa. Peter is real. Peter is here. Found at last. And Peter looks most affa happy as we travel home together, back to the house, for dinner.

Chapter Fifty-two

My long lost friend is so impressed with everything: the kitchen and all the downstairs rooms. I dinna take him upstairs, though Michael disappears up there real quick, as soon as we get home.

"You've done well for yourself, Elizabeth," says Peter, looking at the fancy plates in the cabinet.

"It's Michael's house remember, nae mine."

"Aye, but you're running it, ruling the roost, aren't you?"

"I widna say that," I tell him, and then I detail what Michael said about sending us both home to Scotland, adding that I'd rather pay it all myself, with my share of this year's profit.

Peter is astonished by the whole idea; his mouth hangs open for a bitty before he speaks, and then it's me that's astonished.

"I've only another couple of years left on my indentures," he says. "And then I'm getting money and a bit of land. I'd rather make my fortune here before I go back to Aberdeen."

It's my turn to stand with my mouth agape.

"But you should go, Elizabeth," he continues. "Go and tell everyone what the magistrates did. Call them to answer for their actions. That needs doing." And he proceeds to list names and events, and overheard conversations which he then insists I write down to take back with me as proof.

So. Two men are now really keen to get me on a boat and away from these shores. And away from them. I write down all the names that are dictated to me, and then march back through to the kitchen, Peter following along.

"I've made food as Scottish as I can make it here," I tell Peter, who is then so impressed with everything that I feel churlish for being upset with him. He is just honest and good hearted. He disna mean he wants rid of me. I ken that as I call Michael down to eat, Michael about who I ken no such thing.

"Oh, fit a fine this is," Peter keeps saying all through the meal until it becomes funny. The broth, the bread, the cheese, the oat bannocks, the ham, the apple pie, the cream: all fine as fine can be.

"It is good to hear the spik of my country again," I say, laughing.

"It's real good to have this meal that is far finer than any I had there or here," says Peter.

"Beth is a wonderful cook," adds Michael, as I get up to prepare our chocolate drink.

"I've never had chocolate," says Peter, eyeing the brown liquid suspiciously.

"Oh you're in for a treat!" I tell him.

But it's clear from the moment Peter tastes the drink that he does not like it, though he tries to hide the fact. Happily for him, the folk from the cook house and the quines arrive at this point to distract us all from the subject.

"These are some of my dearest friends," I tell him. "They took me under their wings when I was first arrived, when I didna ken anything about how things were here. And these are the quines I met in the forest!"

"Well, I do like to be in a roomful of quines," says Peter, then proceeding to charm everyone with his witty and open disposition.

There's one awkward moment when he asks Hannah if she's a real bonefide Red Indian and she tells him that she is Lenape.

"Your people's been treated real bad by the British," says Peter. "There's trouble brewing I hear."

Hannah just nods, but any offence she may have taken before is gone.

"You're a nice lad, Peter," says Rebecca.

"You'll make someone a fine husband one of these days," adds Nivvie, and Mary giggles.

"Well it won't be me," I tell them. "All the men hereabouts are desperate to get rid of me on a boat back to Scotland as soon as possible!"

"No one wants rid of you, Beth," says Michael so quietly that maybe only I hear him. I think it's about all he says the whole afternoon. I ignore him anyway.

"Well there's a ship docked just now," says Peter. "A fine one, sailing for Aberdeen in two weeks it is."

"See?" I say to the room, acting jovial, though the 'two weeks' part has sent me into some sort of inner spinning reel, like I'm being flung around in a dance that's going far faster than I can cope with.

"Aye Beth, I'm serious," says Peter.

"Oh, I ken ye are!"

"No listen. It's meant to be a good sturdy ship, and hae a decent captain, not like yon we dealt with afore. And there should be cheap passages going. You could come into town to find out about it this week. I'll meet you, see you right."

I laugh and say: "Actually putting me onto the boat himself!" But I'm nae laughing inside.

We walk down to the plantation to show Peter all around, well most of us do. Not Michael. He remains in the house. Peter stays right until dusk, and then Michael drives him home.

I sit out to watch for any late in the season fireflies, wanting to see them all gold against the blue-green gloam that the air and sky take on as evening deepens. We have gloam in Scotland of course. We have trees, bonny bonny forests full of them. But they're not quite like these. They don't look the same. They don't smell the same. The trees here are so large, they're like giant's legs with their feet planted in the earth, so high and so strong and so... oh I dinna ken. What's the point of looking at them? I'm going to be ripped away from everything I know again soon enough.

And no fireflies rise tonight.

Chapter Fifty-three

It's happening. It's really happening. I keep telling myself this fact. Because it is a fact. It's really happening. And I still can't seem to believe it. But it's real. I went with Peter to the docks. I saw the ship. I bought my passage to Scotland. I have the piece of paper in my room. I keep looking at it, to check, you ken, that it's all real.

The paper is real, as are my other papers, and I've gathered a fair few since being in this land. There's the written account of my share of this year's plantation profit. There's the indenture paper that Michael freed me, or Betty McKay, from. And on the very bottom of the pile, I find that silly advertisement for a play, with the word Trewelove on it. Well, that wisna true after all, was it? Blowing all round me as it did when Peter had just disappeared, just before Mrs Sour purchased me. It annoys me to see it now, to be made to think about these things again, so I go and put it in the fire, and remind myself that I am soon to be leaving these shores. I am going home. And that is very very real. Even though it doesn't feel it.

Maybe it's just that it's happening so fast. It's a shock to my mind and my heart. Aye, that's fit it'll be. By the time I go, in two weeks, it'll all seem normal then.

"This is the saddest I've seen you since you got here," Nivvie tells me as we knead bread in the cook house. I'm keeping busy you see, trying to make things seem normal.

"Well, that's not true," I say. "Remember Culloden? And hearing about my father? This is nothing like that."

"That was the grief about people you love dying and being harmed," she says, all wise like. "This is different. You don't have to go, you know."

"Of course I do. It's what I've wanted since I got here. To find Peter. To get home. It's just… I've a lot of friends to miss now."

Aye. That's fit it is. I decide to start saying goodbye to them all, to bless these friendships with a parting word, said with plenty time given to each, rather than in haste just as I'm leaving.

The quines are still camped nearby so I give them back the Elf Blade. Hannah returns the now well-worn leather bracelet. We're both happy with the exchange, but nae really with the finality of the parting. There's just not a lot of happiness about in these parts right now.

A couple of days later Hannah finds me and returns the blade, though she doesn't want the bracelet back. "It is a stone of Scotland," she says of the old arrowhead. "It wants to go home to Scotland. I wish you are not going."

"Aye, well," I say, pocketing the wretched pin. "You're the only one."

"No. I am not," she says to me, in perfect English, before turning and running back into the trees.

I ride into town and go to Mr Franklin's shop. He's there and I tell him I'm going. He says he'll really miss the chocolate sales and then peers at me directly through his spectacles. "And Michael will miss you," he says.

"I don't think so," I tell him.

"Maybe you should devote some more time to thinking, my dear."

I shake my head at the cheek of him but do stock up on chocolate for Michael, and buy some for Sarah and Comfort too, before visiting them.

"You're really going?" says Sarah, and she sounds cross.

"Of course I'm going."

"Now Sarah…" says Comfort.

"Well!" says she. "It's like the girl's not got eyes in her head."

Comfort walks me to the door as I'm leaving. "Nobody knows, you know."

"Knows what?"

"About Michael," he says, pausing a moment before going on. "About the family. He looks white, Beth. Two white parents. No one would question it. And even if they did, not a one could prove it. You, he… you could do what you want and it would be nobody else's business."

Uncertain how to reply to this, I just say, "Aye Comfort, for sure," and then hug him tightly before leaving.

I am going to miss the old man something fierce, him having been the father figure of my home for the last four years. He was certainly coming out with some random, nonsensical things today though, I think as I wipe a tear away. Older people can be a bit queer like that at times. I wonder how Eppy and Jock are. There's no point me writing to tell them I'm coming, for the letter would be travelling on the same ship as me anyway.

I ride my – well, Michael's – mare into the woods to see Mr Lay. And he is queerer yet than Comfort and Sarah and Mr Franklin.

"You must think about the essence of what you want," he says.

"I've wanted to find Peter and go home since I got here." Why do I have to keep explaining this to people? It's most affa vexing.

"Oh yes," he says, nodding. "You found Peter, and he's doing well, and you have experienced happiness around this."

I nod too. Some sense is being talked at last.

"But going back to Scotland is different," he says.

"Well obviously it's a bit different," I admit.

"I could say I want to have a delicious meal," says Mr Lay. "Someone might give me a plate of roast beef. I would not be happy. But to others, to the world, it would seem as if had what I wanted."

"Scotland is not a plate of roast beef."

"But ask yourself: is this choice going to bring me something akin to the fresh and delicious vegetables that Mr Lay craves? Does it provide for the true longings of my heart?"

I frown. I'm feeling something strange about this, his words. "Scotland is my heart, a big bit of my heart."

"You want to go home, Beth," he says. "Think on this with much seriousness as you choose the next bend in your path."

Old people! Annoyed as I am with Michael, it is a relief to journey back to him, after leaving the gift of fresh vegetables from my garden with Mr Lay. Hopefully it will provide for the true longings of his heart.

I make an apple pie. I feel deeply sad for Michael, about Michael. We hardly speak anymore, and while I am cross that he wants me gone, I am most definitely going to miss him. In fact, it hurts my heart so much, I dinna want to think about it.

I've got to start preparing myself to go. To really go. There's fear in me about the boat, of course there is, what it'll be like, who will be on it. I won't have a friend with me this time. But a far bigger matter is the pain I feel about all the folk, and dogs, and horses, and even bears that I'm leaving. But I canna let them be the focus of my heart. I have to fill it up with Scotland. That is my path. Maybe Mr Lay is not so mad and old after all. I have to think about home. I have to prepare myself for what and who awaits there.

Jock and Eppy. I hope and pray that they are still around, else I will be stuck with Cousin Matthew. There's others nearby that I ken of course. All the farmers on the estate. I wonder how they are faring under their new landlord?

I think about their farms, all freshly ploughed as they probably are now. Has the first frost iced the chocolatey brown earth with white sparkle yet? I think about the pink castle walls, they have a wee bit of sparkle to them too, and the ancient stone circle and the old oak wood. The path through the oaks will be covered in their fallen shapely leaves now, all green and yellow and brown. These are the things I must fill my heart and head with as I sweep and cook and garden. I want to leave the garden neat. I dinna ken if Michael will get a new cook, or if he'll go to live with Comfort and Sarah, or maybe he'll just get fed by the cook house folks.

I see him, standing outside, looking over at the pink sky above the trees of the forest. His shoulders are sloped. He's not enjoying this time either. Well, it will soon be over.

And before we hardly have time to think about it anyway, it is.

Chapter Fifty-four

The sound of the dogs barking and whining is unbearable. They ken. And there's nothing I can do to comfort them, so I just cover my ears as we drive away. Michael is driving. I am just sitting.

"They'll be all right," he says.

"Aye. I ken." I do ken. Michael will look after them, and they will look after him, but I canna think on that. I focus on Scotland. Oak leaves on an old path. Not fireflies rising up out of the green and into the night. Their season is all but finished now anyway. And I will never see them again. Ever. No! That's the sort of thought I can't bear. So I start up a different conversation involving nothing sad. In fact it's mundane.

"What do you think you'll have for supper?" I ask my quiet companion.

"Oh," he says as if distracted from some other very important thought. "Probably just some bread and cheese."

"That's not a proper dinner. There's stew. You ken that there is."

He nods. He better eat the stew. I'll be most cross if he disna. But I'll be on the boat. I winna ken. But I'll be wondering.

"What do you think you'll get on the ship?" he asks. What a fascinating discourse we do share, as we approach the end of our time together.

I think back to the voyage that brought me here. "Ship's biscuits with worms in. Och no, it'll probably be a bit better than that on this boat. At least to start with. And I've got some bread and cheese and apples with me."

"That's not a proper dinner Beth," he says which is just sheer and utter cheek, but it helps somehow. It's a wee bit of humour between the two of us, like we haven't shared in what feels like a long time, but really is just weeks. Two weeks. But it's good that this is how we'll part.

The journey to the docks is over terribly quick. We stop. Michael ties the horse and I realise something is coming over me. Something bad. Something big. Something that's making my cheeks burn as I struggle not to cry.

I can see the boat, all big and grand at the quay. I ken where I've to go. I don't have much with me, just the one bag. I don't need help carrying it. So this is it. This is goodbye.

"Michael…" I don't know what to say. I can remember all the times he's held me, and I've held him, and how we've helped each other in the last four years. The Laudanum. The time after Culloden. The gaol. That Christmas at Sarah's house. These things, these moments, have been missing from my mind in recent weeks. And now they're overwhelming, wrapped all around me like the plaid he gave me. And there are no words that can express all that I'm feeling in the time we've got here before the ship sails.

But he's saving me from having to speak. He's speaking instead. He's holding a paper out to me. He took it from his pocket.

"Don't read it until you are on the boat," he says. "Until it's sailed. Promise me, Beth."

I take it. I tuck it into my bag. It's not making me feel any better and I dinna want to think about it. I put my hands on his chest and look up into his brown eyes. This is it. This is us. The very end.

That big something that was coming over me breaks free and this is what I'm doing: I'm pulling Michael's head down to me and I'm kissing him full on the mouth. Like a harpy. Or a loose woman. But it's nae like that. It's nae like that, and it's nae like anything I've felt before. I feel soft and hot and cold all at once. It's nae just my cheeks that are burning; it's every bit of me. And he kisses me too, his hands on my shoulders. And then on my face. And it's too much. It's more than any one woman can cope with. I want to hold him tighter. I want to pull him closer. I want more of his kiss. So, of course, I run away.

I run past people selling fruit and vegetables in a wee market on the quayside. I run past other passengers getting ready to board. I run past sailor mannies and the very boat I'm going on. I run round the back of a pile of wooden crates, and I crouch there like a wild creature who's been cornered or hunted.

Cry isn't the right word for what I'm doing. This is that sobbing thing I did after I heard of battles lost and lives destroyed. This is grief. It is unbearable and terrible, and I want to feel cross again, to feel better, so I take out Michael's letter, break the seal and tear it open right there, sitting right down onto the ground, hoping that it is annoying enough to make me angry, for that would be better.

My Dearest Dear, it begins. Well that disna help! It's a few minties before I can see to read again. And then it gets worse. The absolute complete and utter cheek and impudence of Michael Sauer!

I know you think I want to send you away, Beth. And it's true. I do want to send you away. Because that is what's best for you. It's how you will have the best life.

If you had stayed here I would have wanted to ask you to marry me. And that's not possible. Not for us. I am not a white man. Oh, I know, or ken as you would say, that that's not the way you think. You dinna separate folks off into their colours. But it is how the world thinks. And black and white cannot marry. Not here. There are laws against it.

So what would happen to you and me if you were staying here? Would we jump the broom? Live in sin? Be despised wherever we go? That's not what I choose for you.

I choose your castle and your forests and your stones for you. You'll find a good Scottish man to marry and have lots of wee fiery headed bairns. And be happy.

Maybe you don't feel the same way as I do. But sometimes I think you do. Sometimes I know you do. But you are headstrong. You would let your heart lead you places that I cannot let myself believe would be the best for you.

But know that in my heart I did not want to send you away, I did not want you to go. I love you with every part of my being. And I always will.

Michael.

Chapter Fifty-five

I've reached a blank state. I passed though extreme anger quite quickly. Fury. Wanting to shout and rage. Then I cried a bit more. And now I'm here. By the ship. The great and glorious ship that will carry me home. It's a lot nicer than The Planter. I can see that. I study the painted blue side of the vessel and the gang plank. Even it, the gang plank, is nicer than that of The Planter, the one I let myself be tricked into walking over.

I dinna walk over this one right away, though there are no tricks here. I step aside to let other people pass. I'm still blank. I'm not ready to show my paper of passage. Or board the boat. A family go by me: a mother, a father and a wee loon. The child does remind me of Thomas, my brother Thomas, and I'm cast back in time, remembering how happy and full of love and laughter the castle was before he died. It was a warm home then. My home. It was cold and empty after that. Tiptoeing around being quiet. It was full of so many people I loved and then, overnight, it wasn't. They went away or went to sleep.

I can feel my love for Thomas in my heart, all warm and glowy. And my father. Even my mother, poor wretch that she was. Love. Love. Lots of love.

I remember standing on an ancient Scottish stone and dreaming of love and adventure, of fireflies and chocolate even.

I walk back over to the market area of the quay and buy an onion from the people selling vegetables. I hold the onion in my hand and study it. Its wee stubby roots, growing no more. Plucked out of friendly soil. American soil. I stare at the onion and remember one just like it. In Scotland. I cut that one up real clumsy and fast, so vexed was I about something that really didn't matter at all. It was part of the last meal I made there. I recall, too, the onion that was part of the first meal I made here. In the kitchen, as Michael and Mrs Sour shouted away at each other upstairs. That's when I decided to stay, when I was looking down at that little round vegetable, just as I am now.

I'm ready to take the next steps on my path. Still holding the onion, I walk over the gang plank. Still holding the onion, I remember more details of the last time I walked over such a plank onto a ship. There's no sack this time. No being taken or sent anywhere. Just me, moving my own feet, holding my onion, making my own choices.

A young man and woman stand just inside the entrance to the ship, and they're both crying and clutching at each other. It's that kind of day, that kind of place.

"I'll come when I've got the money," says the man.

"Aye," says the woman in the speech of my Scottish home. "But when will that be?" She says the word 'when' like 'phan'. I remember folk speaking like that. I remember it well.

It's clear they don't know when, or phan, their reunion will be. It's clear that it might actually be never. And they love each other, the two of them. That's clear to see. Though he is affa English spoken. That won't go down too well in Aberdeen. But that doesn't matter to them any more than such a thing would ever matter to me.

"Is it the fare you dinna have?" I ask them. "Is that why you canna both go?"

"Aye, quine, fit else?" says the young woman.

Now, I ken fit you're thinking: Elizabeth Manteith, you're still as spoiled as ever, standing there with that onion, all sulky and cross, when you've just been given everything you've wanted for the last four years!

Aye, well. Maybe I am spoiled. But I'm other things too. I'm nae so silly as I was afore I came here to this land. I'm grown. I'm brave. And I'm nae stupid. And I ken one thing above all others: I dinna just want to go home; the Elfin Blade wants to go home, and so it shall, but not with me, for there are others who want to go home, and to be with those they love, just as much as I do. And, for all of us, this desire is greater than a mere want, and I hand over my passage paper to where it has to go.

And now: I need to go home.

I have to go home.

So here I am. The sky is dark but the fire is hot. It will cook my onion tart just fine. I even put cheese on this one, not like that first time when I could only find the most basic ingredients. I trim the edges of the pastry and share them out between my three doggies. They've been sitting gazing up at me for a while now, being most affa good and quiet.

I've kent that he's there for a while now too. But I wisna ready to speak to him until now. I wisna ready to look upon his face until now.

I turn and look straight at him, leaning as he is against the door frame, all handsome and soft looking around the eyes and nearly smiling.

And before I tell him that I do want those red headed babies, and that I will not have him or anyone else choose what is right for me, and that Scotland may claim part of my heart but he owns the bigger share, being, in fact, my true love who I used to dream of meeting, I just say the simplest thing, the plainest truth of all: "I've come home."

Historical Notes

This story was inspired by the six hundred children and young people who were kidnapped from Aberdeen during the 1740s and sold into indentured servitude in the American colonies. Most of the accounts from this time were written by men, and wanting to explore a female perspective, I created Elizabeth Manteith, borne from the family featured in *The Mermaid and the Bear*. Peter Williamson, Benjamin Lay and Benjamin Franklin were all real people as were Alexander Young and Captain Ragg. Hannah, I named for Hannah Freeman, a woman who became known as the Last Lenape or Indian Hannah, though the character in these pages is entirely fictional.

I have played a little fast and loose with Peter's age. He was actually only 13 years old when kidnapped in 1743. Given that he stretched the truth somewhat in his own writings, describing himself as 'an infant' at this time, rather than the strapping lad he was, I think he might forgive me my adjustment in favour of the story. He returned to Aberdeen many years later, having written a book about his experiences in which he accused the local magistrates of involvement in the kidnappings. His book was burnt at the Mercat Cross in town and he was imprisoned for a while in the Tolbooth (now a museum). He eventually travelled to Edinburgh and took up a case against the Aberdeen magistrates, and won.

The Planter sailed from Aberdeen with its cargo of children and furniture on May 12th 1743. A girl was found dead in First Mate Alexander Young's bunk during the voyage. The shipwreck happened as written, including the temporary desertion of some of the children and the three weeks on the island.

The following books proved invaluable in writing this story.

Peter Williamson, *The Life and Curious Adventures of Peter Williamson, Who was Carried off from Aberdeen and Sold for a Slave*, York, 1757

Douglas Skelton, *Indian Peter, The Extraordinary Life and Adventures of Peter Williamson*, Mainstream Publishing Company (Edinburgh) Ltd, 2004

Benjamin Lay 1677 - 1759, *A Pioneer Quaker Anti-Slavery Abolitionist and Activist*, Joshua Evans' Trust 2015

Dawn G. Marsh, *A Lenape Among The Quakers, The Life of Hannah Freeman*, The Board of Regents of The University of Nebraska, 2014

Maggie Craig, *Damn Rebel Bitches*, Mainstream Publishing, 2000

Carol Berkin and Leslie Horowitz (ed.), *Women's Voices, Women's Lives*, Northeastern University Press, 1998

Ann Chandonnet, *Colonial Food*, Shire Publications, 2013